James Grant

The Cameronians

A Novel

James Grant

The Cameronians
A Novel

ISBN/EAN: 9783337003289

Printed in Europe, USA, Canada, Australia, Japan

Cover: Foto ©Andreas Hilbeck / pixelio.de

More available books at **www.hansebooks.com**

THE CAMERONIANS.

A Novel.

BY

JAMES GRANT,

AUTHOR OF

'THE ROMANCE OF WAR,' 'OLD AND NEW EDINBURGH,' ETC.

IN THREE VOLUMES.
VOL. I.

LONDON:

RICHARD BENTLEY AND SON,

Publishers in Ordinary to Her Majesty the Queen.

1881.

TO

GEORGE ROUTLEDGE, ESQ.,

MY OLD FRIEND AND PUBLISHER,

I INSCRIBE THIS MILITARY STORY,

AS A TRIBUTE

OF

RESPECT AND ESTEEM.

PREFACE.

THE old Scottish regiment from which the following story takes its title, and of which the hero is described as a member, is on the point of losing its identity, and after the July of this year will be united with the 90th Perthshire Light Infantry, as 'The Scottish Cameronian Rifles,' thus losing, of course, its scarlet uniform, colours, and facings — the royal yellow of Scotland, which, by a correspondence with Mr. Childers, in March last, the author was fortunate enough to secure (instead of buff) for all Scottish infantry, not faced with blue.

Of the merits of the new regimental system it is difficult to speculate as yet; but it will too probably create an endless confusion, and be long a source of regret to the entire army.

25, Tavistock Road,
Westbourne Park.
May, 1881.

CONTENTS OF VOL. I.

THE CAMERONIANS.

CHAPTER I.

EAGLESCRAIG.

'TWENTY - SIXTH Regiment,' said the old general, raising his voice, as he rustled the morning paper importantly, after taking it from the ebony reading-easel (attached to the arm of his large and comfortable velvet easy-chair), whereon Mr. Tunley, the butler, always laid the journals, after he had duly aired and cut them. 'Twenty-sixth Regiment,' he added, coughing and clearing his voice, 'a detachment of this distinguished corps, says the *Ayr Observer*, has recently arrived at the castle of Dumbarton, under the command of Lieutenants Cecil Falconer and Leslie Fotheringhame.'

'Well, there is nothing remarkable in that, uncle,' said one of his young lady listeners, who seemed chiefly intent upon her breakfast, and not much interested by the intelligence.

'My old regiment—my old regiment still,' said the old man, musingly. 'Gad, I'll have the senior—what's his name? Cecil Falconer—over here, for a few days' cover-shooting.'

'And why not the other too?' asked the young lady who had just spoken, laughingly; 'we might have an admirer each, Annabelle.'

But Miss Erroll, to whom the name of Fotheringhame seemed not unknown, coloured and did not reply.

'Both could not leave their men at the same time,' said the general.

'Then I hope the senior is a pleasant fellow—he whom you propose to bring, Sir

Piers,' said Mr. Hew Montgomerie, of whom more anon.

'All the Cameronians were pleasant fellows in *my* time,' said the general, tartly, 'and I have no doubt they are so still. And remember, girls, that the smartest officers are usually selected for detachment duty,' he added.

Those remarks passed in the cosy and elegant morning-room of Eaglescraig, the mansion of Sir Piers Montgomerie, Bart., who—a retired general officer—was G.C.B. and G.C.S.I. and Colonel of the Cameronian Regiment, and Governor of the Castle of Dumbarton: and the party at breakfast consisted only of Sir Piers, his remote kinsman and heir, Hew Montgomerie, of the Indian Civil Service, home on a year's leave ; his grandniece and orphan ward Mary, also a Montgomerie ; her friend Annabelle Erroll —both very handsome girls—and an old lady who presided over the silver tea-urn and Wedgewood breakfast equipage, Mrs. Garth, Mary's governess and friend, the widow of an old captain of the Cameronians—five personages, with whom we hope to make the reader fully acquainted in time.

Sir Piers was verging now on his seventieth year, but he was fresher and more hale and hearty than many a man of fifty. His features were still handsome and regular, though lined and wrinkled ; his eyes were keen as those of a hawk, and his figure, still wonderfully erect, was clad in a rich maroon - coloured robe-de-chambre, with yellow silk facings, cord, and tassels, and he was seated near the blazing winter fire, with his feet on a velvet stool, and encased in slippers of Mary's handiwork.

Generous by nature, yet hot-tempered and proud—pride of birth had been a positive vice with him in early life—Sir Piers was a curious mixture of the testy old Indian general, accustomed to every luxury, including tyrannising over ' niggers,' with the country gentleman of the old school ; and having a profound admiration for the service and everything pertaining thereto, like old Bismarck, he believed that every man should be a soldier and rejoice in being one.

In his latter years Sir Piers had not been with the Cameronians, but had seen a deal of service in India as a general officer, and, while slowly creeping up the list of his rank, had been appointed, in the usual courtesy of the army, full colonel of the old regiment in which he had been a sub-altern and field-officer.

His hunting-days were well-nigh past now; yet, at a meet, all the field rejoiced to see the fine old man in his saddle, and with all his pride of bearing—for a wealthy *parvenu*, however honestly he had won his wealth, Sir Piers would have treated with chilling hauteur—he was never above con-versing with some sturdy farmer of Kyle or Cunninghame, kindly and affably, on the price of stock, the fall of wheat, on breed-ing, fattening, or draining, and always winding up by some, often irrelevant, anecdote of his sporting experiences in India, or when he followed the drums of the Cameronians. Old as he was, he had

never been known to shrink from a bull-
finch, or be fished out of a brook; he was
welcome in every homestead throughout the
country-side, and the farmers' wives always
assumed their brightest looks, brought
forth their whitest tablecloths and the best
contents of larder and pantry, in honour of
the old Laird of Eaglescraig, when he
came their way.

He was a Justice of the Peace and Com-
missioner of Supply for the County; he
read the *Field*, of course, as what country
gentleman does not? He studied the War
Office *Gazette* regularly, as if he expected
his own name to appear there, once weekly;
he was simple in all his tastes and happy
in all his surroundings, yet, for all that,
there was a skeleton in his house and
heart, known, perhaps, to himself alone.

He was a childless man now—childless
by an act of his own—and the title and
estates, which he inherited from a long line
of ancestors, were eventually to pass from
him to the heir of entail, whom he strove
hard, but in vain, to like or admire.

The latter, Hew Caddish Montgomerie, was then about thirty years of age. He was not ungentlemanly either in manner or bearing; but his face, like his disposition, was very defective. His eyes were called grey, and seemed to be grey at times; yet, on closer inspection, it was but too apparent that those shifty and furtive orbs of his were of different colours, for one was a species of bilious green.

They were closely set on each side of a nose that strongly resembled a shoe-horn, and his mouth, which was both cruel and licentious in contour, was partly concealed, or altered in expression, by a luxuriant brown moustache. He had come home, we have said, on leave from the C. S., a sharp hand at cards and with a billiard-cue, deeply dipped in debt, and with the current reputation, among his set, of being 'a bad lot.' His mother, daughter of a Sudder judge, was one of the old English family of Caddish, a name which Hew was wont to affirm was a corruption of Cavendish; be that as it may, the corruption thereof, in some instances, suited his character amazingly well.

'This is rather unlike your usual proud exclusiveness, Sir Piers,' said he, after a pause.

'What? inviting this young officer to knock over a few birds?'

'Yes—without an introduction.'

'Introduction? None was needed in *my* time; the epaulettes were introduction enough everywhere. The service is certainly *not* what it was in my day, the special school of honour and politeness; but I'll do the right thing, for all that. Let me see, which is senior—Falconer or Fotheringhame. Tunley, hand me the "Army List." Thanks. It *is* Falconer. I have known what it is to be on detachment in such a dull hole as Dumbarton, killing time till the spring drills come on, so I'll invite the senior.'

'And how about the poor junior?' asked Miss Erroll, colouring slightly again.

'Well, even to gratify you, Annabelle, I cannot bring him,' said the general, laugh-

ing. 'I remember once, when we were in
cantonments at Barrackpore——' Hew
smiled as the general began thus ; but they
were spared the probably prosy reminiscence,
for just then Sir Piers' faded features
clouded suddenly, as he put down the
'Army List' and said, in a changed voice :
'Had my boy Piers lived, he might now
have been at the head of the regiment—
five-and-twenty years ago—five-and-twenty
years ! My God, how long—how time has
rolled away !'

His eyes, as he thought this, rather
than spoke it all aloud, were cast for a
moment furtively—as if he was ashamed
of exhibiting any sudden emotion—on the
full-length portrait of a handsome young
subaltern, in the uniform of the Cameronians, scarlet faced with yellow, massive
gold epaulettes, and the silver sphinx on
his belt-plate. It represented a spirited-
looking young fellow with a proud and
joyous expression of face, and a well-knit,
well-set-up figure.

The shifty, parti-coloured eyes of Hew

Montgomerie travelled for a moment in the same direction, **and then** he addressed himself **to** the grouse-pie, thinking the while that 'things were deucedly well ordered as they were, **so** far as *he* was concerned.' And then the meal proceeded somewhat silently, Mrs. Garth officiating over **the cups,** and Mr. Tunley, a paragon of old rubicund butlers, at the side-board, where the cold beef and grouse-pie **were** placed, among **Indian** jars and old silver race tankards.

Mary Montgomerie, the general's grand-niece **and** ward, **and her** chief friend and gossip, Annabelle **Erroll, were both** attractive **and** very handsome girls, each in her **twentieth** year, but different in their styles and complexions.

Of a good stature, and round, firm and graceful in **form,** Mary Montgomerie had well-defined eyebrows, eyes, and hair, all of the darkest **brown**; long lashes lent a great softness to her white-lidded eyes, and she **had a** quiet ease, elegance, and girlish innocence of manner; yet at times she was full of vivacity, born of the fact or knowledge that she had been, as an orphan, from her youth, much of a petted child, and reminded by many around her that she was the heiress of many a thousand and many an acre, provided that she wedded with the full approval of one who was not likely to be severe upon her—old Sir Piers, her grand-uncle and legal guardian; for she was the only daughter of his favourite younger brother—younger by several years.

As such she filled a void in his heart, and ever and anon the old man's eyes were wont to rest kindly, fondly, and admiringly upon her.

Her complexion was fair and creamy, her features regular and minute, yet they were hardly ever in repose, for every variety of expression, as thought inspired it, flitted over the ever-changing face.

Though less favoured by fortune, and even by nature, her friend Miss Erroll was nevertheless a charming girl of the blonde type, with grey-blue eyes and fair hair shot with gold, as it seemed, in

the sunlight, soft, plentiful, and wavy as
the darker tresses of Mary, and her eyebrows and their lashes were just a shade
darker than her hair. In the tone and
tenour of her ways she was less impulsive
than Mary Montgomerie, who at times
would come down the house stairs at a
headlong rush, while Annabelle followed
with calm step and slow, or would quietly
seek a gate in the hunting-field, while
Mary, with her horse's head uplifted by
her light, unerring hand, cleared the nearest
hedge at a flying leap, and with a laugh
that rang like a merry silver bell.

Both girls were eminently graceful and
full of charming manners and pretty winning words and ways ; but the difference of
their temperaments was indicated even by
the style of their morning-dresses, for the
robe of Annabelle was pale blue, as became
the character of her beauty, while that of
Mary was of warm maize colour, tied with
fluttering scarlet ribbons, with rosettes of
the same to match on her tiny slippers.
The loose, wide, falling sleeves of this gar-

ment coquettishly showed her round white arm at times, from the taper wrist to the dimpled elbow, and then she would smile and hastily let them fall forward when she caught the quick, shifty eyes of Hew Montgomerie cast admiringly on her.

The fifth of our *dramatis personæ*, as yet, is Mrs. Griselda Garth, or, as she preferred to be called with the old Scoto-French courtesy, that is now passing away, 'Mrs. Captain Garth.' The widow of a Cameronian officer who had died on service in the East, a calm, subdued, and gentle, white-haired old lady, she had found now, for life, a quiet home at Eaglescraig, and had acted for more than twelve years as a species of tender mother to Mary; and thus, after her duties as a governess were past, she remained as her mentor, companion, and chaperon, honoured, loved, and trusted by Mary and old Sir Piers, who had been her husband's friend.

'If Mr. Falconer avails himself of my invitation, and I don't see very well how he can decline it,' said the latter, returning to his late idea, and viewing it somewhat in the light of a regimental order, 'the dog-cart can meet him at the Montgomerie Arms in Ardrossan; and you, Hew, will do me the favour to drive him here to Eaglescraig.'

'Yes; that will be in better taste than sending a servant,' added Mary.

'Excuse me, Sir Piers,' said Hew, almost sulkily, as his chronic jealousy already took the alarm; 'but I don't care for acting as charioteer to a total stranger.'

'As you please,' replied Sir Piers haughtily, as he always disliked to have his wishes thwarted; 'some one else will obey my orders, I have no doubt.'

Eaglescraig, in the Bailiwick of Cunninghame, we may describe as a magnificent modern villa, with plate-glass oriels, a pillared portico, a stately perron, and balustraded terrace, whereon the peacocks spread their plumes and strutted to and fro. It had been, somewhat incongruously we must admit, added to, or engrafted on, the tall, old, square baronial tower that for ages had been, from the lofty bluff known as the Eaglescraig, a landmark of the sea, and which started up gaunt and grim, with grated windows, corbelled battlements, and tourelles at the angles—a tower the pride of the general's heart as the cradle of his house, and the home of his ancestors, all unsuited though it was to modern usages, taste, and requirements— an edifice so massive and old, that Hardy Knute, when he dwelt in the adjacent castle of Glengarnock, may have shared in it the hospitality of that Sir Hew Montgomerie who fought at the battle of Largs, and whose coat-of-arms, three *fleurs-de-lis*, with three *annulets* quarterly, crested by a maiden holding a man's head, may still be seen above its northern door; and these Sir Piers had now reproduced upon everything else, from the carriage panels to the dogs' collars and the salt-spoons.

On one side the house of Eaglescraig commanded a view which, on a summer day, was a delightful one, when there was just breeze enough to swell the passing

sails—the glorious **Firth of Clyde, with**
the dark-blue **peaks of** Arran in the dis-
tance, widening out into the ocean, with
ships homeward bound after many a tedious,
rough, or prosperous voyage ; others with
their prows turned towards the far horizon,
bearing **with** them, perhaps, expatriated
Highland emigrants, their hearts filled
with sorrow and regret, rather than with the
thoughts **of** ' high emprise,' so necessary
for an **exile's** success in the doubtful
future.

Close in shore, below the beetling cliff,
when the wind is from the land, may
be seen **the** many coasting vessels and
steamers plying to and fro, shooting clear,
as if by magic, from many **a** rocky pro-
montory and bluff, where, **thick** as gnats,
the sea-birds wheel **and** scream ; and in
many **a** sheltered **cove** the boats, brown-
tarred and clinker-built, moored or safely
beached, for the people there are all hardy
and thrifty fisher-folk.

But on the landward side the view was
different, and there the eye could wander

over the tolerably flat and very fertile acres of Sir Piers Montgomerie, wood, wold and pasture, the richest part, perhaps, of the rich dairy-farm producing land in a district of which, as the old rhyme says:

> ' Kyle for a man,
>   And Carrick for a coo;
>   *Cunninghame* for butter and cheese,
>   And Galloway for woo'.'

So the general's invitation to Lieutenant Cecil Falconer was written by Mary and despatched, to the great annoyance of Hew, and all in Eaglescraig knew that in another day or two the recipient thereof, who had accepted it, was coming.

Mary Montgomerie and her friend Annabelle Erroll were too much accustomed to society, and the gaiety of fashionable life, to feel even any girlish excitement at the prospect of a young sub being added to their present small circle at Eaglescraig; nevertheless, in the seclusion of their dressing-closet, it was voted and passed by them, *nem. con.*, that the said addition would not be unacceptable; and, on lot being laughingly cast as to whom he should fall a victim, the prize was Mary's.

And after this they ceased to think upon the subject—certainly, at least, so far as the latter lady was concerned.

CHAPTER II.

HEW'S LOVE-MAKING.

DURING the few days that passed before the arrival of the expected guest at Eaglescraig, Hew was more than usually attentive to the general's wealthy ward; and one forenoon when they were idling in the long avenue, which led through the Dovecot Park down the woodland slope towards the highway, he resolved, if possible, to bring matters to a successful issue with her.

For fully a month past, since his appearance at Eaglescraig, Mary had been used to this love-making of his, apparently,

as she treated him half coquettishly, and
yet so 'chaffingly,' that — but for his
extreme vanity, or obtuseness—he must
have seen that he had no chance of
success.

Mary valued his attentions at their real
worth, and times there were when he eyed
her gloomily—yea, angrily, for he trusted
more in Sir Piers' influence, wishes, and
authority, to bend her to his will, than to
any merit of his own.

Thus his love-making was a curious com-
bination of earnestness, banter, and sullenness ; earnestness caused by the girl's great
beauty, which he certainly valued, and her
great wealth, which he valued much more,
on one hand ; and on the other, genuine
dislike of India, with his own impecunious
circumstances, and a knowledge of Sir
Piers' wishes.   The banter came at times,
because he was really incapable of loving
any girl truly ; and the sullenness was born
of his lack of success, with a chronic
jealousy of every other man who addressed
her.

On this forenoon in the Dovecot Park,
Annabelle Erroll did not accompany them,
so Hew proceeded to utilise the occasion.

Mary looked bewitchingly beautiful and
piquante in her rich brown sealskin, a
grey skirt and a coquettish black velvet
hat with a scarlet feather. She kept her
hands obstinately in her tiny muff; thus
Hew had no pretence for capturing one of
them in any way as a suggestive pre-
liminary to something more, and could
only walk by her side and utter his soft
nothings from time to time, to which she
listened, half amused and half bored the
while, and not helping him in any way.

The winter day was clear and bright,
and the keen gusty breeze that swept
from the sea over Eaglescraig imparted a
rosebud tint to Mary's usually pale cheeks
that enhanced her beauty by adding a
fresh light to her eyes. The gusts of
wind whirled showers of yellow and brown
leaves across the sward, and drifts of
stormy clouds through the sky over land
and Firth, yet Mary's spirits were a

high pressure, and though but little sunshine lit the December landscape, she was
full of merriment and the *espiègleric* that
were natural to her.

The dovecot they were approaching,
like most of the ancient edifices of that
kind in Scotland, was built in the form of
an enormous beehive, some twenty feet
high, and full of columbaria for the pigeons,
which were flying in clouds around it, or
perched on the summit thereof. It was,
in due conformity to an ancient act of the
Scottish Parliament, placed in the very
centre of the Montgomerie estate, so that
the birds should not prey upon the corn of
other proprietors; and the reason why so
many of these antique dovecots in Scotland survive the mansions to which they
belonged, is supposed to be an old superstition, that if the dovecot is destroyed,
the lady of the land dies within the
year.

Near that of Eaglescraig are two large
yellow rings or circles strongly marked in
the green-sward (like those on the hill of

Craiganrarie), drawn by the sword of an
evil Montgomerie, who had trafficked in
Satanic influence, and thus had formed round
him an orbit of protection, before summon-
ing his sable majesty, and round which the
latter had to keep running, so long as he
was visible to mortal eyes.

'You do worry me, Hew,' said Mary,
with something of a saucy laugh, 'and I
have every mind to stand in the conjuror's
circle and defy you to approach me.'

'Do you deem me, then, so distasteful,
so odious, and such an incarnation of evil?'

'No; but seriously, what is the aim, the
object of all this attention, Cousin Hew?
for though the tie is a remote one certainly,
I may call you cousin, I believe.'

'Do, dearest Mary.'

'Well?' she asked, curtly and impatiently.

'The aim and object, you say?'

'Yes, yes.'

'To marry you, of course; that is—that
is, if you will have me, and please Sir
Piers,' he replied, with perfect deliberation

and more apparent coolness than he usually felt.

'I won't consult grand-uncle on *that* matter, Cousin Hew. Besides, now that I think of it, I don't want to marry.'

'Indeed! I thought marriage was the sole aim of every girl's existence.'

'In novels more than in real life, perhaps. Besides, marriage is only to be thought of when the man and the hour come.'

'It is the end of all anxieties,' urged Hew, who thought no doubt of his monetary ones.

'I have none to end; and with many girls it is only the beginning of a set of troubles which none of them expect. But let us drop this very funny conversation.'

'Why?'

'You surely would not seek a wife with half a heart, or none!'

'The half of your heart, Mary, is worth the whole of any other woman's!' replied Hew, with more warmth and gallantry than he had yet shown; but the provoking

Mary only laughed, and as she drew near the dovecot, some of the pigeons, to whom her figure was familiar, and whom she was wont to bring food for, came wheeling and fluttering round her, and one, after nestling in her neck—a pretty sight—alighted on her left hand, and while she stroked and fed it with the right, Hew could not but remark that the snow-white pigeon was not whiter than her slender fingers.

'I would I were that pigeon,' said he, sentimentally.

'"Would I were a glove upon that hand!"—now don't be a goose and attempt to act Romeo, as I cannot be your Juliet,' said Mary, laughing outright; and now he began to eye her with his gloomiest expression in his parti-coloured orbs, while she caressed the bird, and sang, as if to it, part of Lady Anne Lindsay's song:

'" Why tarries my love ? Ah, where does he roam ?
      My love is long absent from me.
   Come hither, sweet dove, I'll write to my love,
      And send him a letter by thee.

' " Her dove she did deck, she drew o'er his neck
    A bell and a collar so gay ;
  She tied to his wing a scroll with a string,
    Then kissed him and sent him away." '

Suiting the action to the word, she kissed
the pigeon and tossed it from her with a
merry ringing laugh, for she had ever a
light glad heart, and was full of pretty, yet
haughty and winsome ways.

  Hew, in the vanity of his nature, could
not see how hopeless it was for him to press
his suit with a girl who never listened to
him seriously, and who never tried, even in
the least degree, to care for him ; for there
was something in Hew Caddish Montgomerie that made Mary totally indifferent
to all he could urge, and so she felt neither
regret for, nor gratitude to him : thus she
could hear unmoved the avowal and proposal from his lips, which seldom fail to
stir in one way or another the hearts of
most women, and which, whoever utters
them, are seldom or never forgotten.

  ' Let us be friends, Hew,' said she, in
reply to another appeal ; ' I do not love

you—I cannot love you as you wish, and I dare not and would not marry where I did not love.'

Hew eyed her still more gloomily and almost revengefully, while she played with the spray of a wild-rose tree, till a little cry escaped her, as a thorn entered her delicate hand.

'Do permit me, Mary,' he urged, and tenderly enough he extracted the thorn, and bowing over her hand, pressed it to his lips; but Mary almost angrily snatched it away, just as the sound of wheels was heard, and there bowled up the winding avenue a dog-cart, the driver and the occupant of which must have seen, and no doubt misunderstood, the whole situation.

'Our new guest with his gun-case and portmanteaus,' said Hew, with much annoyance.

'Who?' asked Mary, still more annoyed, as she thought of what Hew had done.

'Have you forgotten?'

'Oh! you mean Mr. Cecil Falconer.'

'Yes, that fellow from Dumbarton.

Now don't, please, run off to the house,
Mary; we shall meet him and his military
appetite betimes, no doubt, when the gong
sounds for dinner.'

Mary had now an undefined sense of
provocation, and in silence turned away
towards the house, accompanied by Hew,
who found his chance was gone for that
day, and Mary never gave him another if
it could be avoided.

Thus ere long he began to fear that
until Sir Piers' demise, and the baronetcy
and broad acres of Eaglescraig became his
by succession, he might have to face the
Indian C.S. again; and seek how to meet
his debts by trying—as he had often done—
his fortune at ' the board of green cloth.'

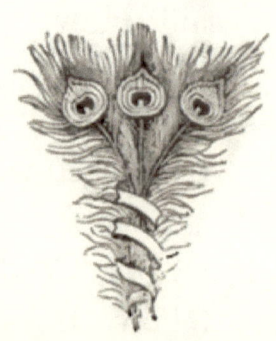

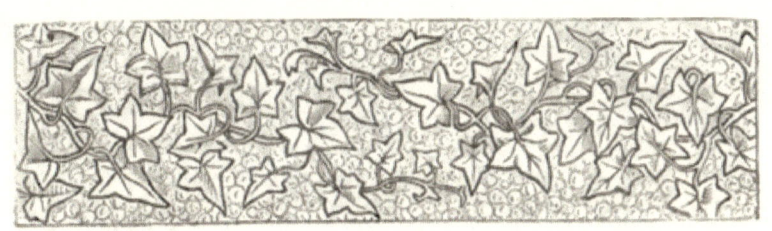

CHAPTER III.

FIRST IMPRESSIONS.

THE sense of having borne a part in a *scene*—an event which is dreaded by well-bred folks—prevented Mary from making her appearance till dinner-time, when, after achieving a most effective toilette, she entered the lighted drawing-room.

Though almost totally unembarrassed by any memory of Hew's absurd love-making, she had nevertheless been provoked that the new guest should have been cognisant of his gallantry in the avenue. She could but hope that he had forgotten it, which was certainly not the case, and ere she had

left her dressing-closet, she paused before
the pier-glass to peep at her own sweet face
and all her bravery, ere she swept away
down the great staircase to the drawing-
room, where already the general and their
visitor were on the best of terms, laughing
and, as Mrs. Garth phrased it, 'talking
shop in full swing.'

'Yes, yes,' she heard Sir Piers saying, 'it
was there at the storming of that hill-fort
that the notable dispute took place between
Douglas of "Ours" and Bruce of the Bengal
Infantry, as to which was senior and *who*
should lead the stormers; till Douglas,
when the bullets, egad! were flying like
hail down the breach, lowered his sword
and said, "When a Bruce is to lead, a
Douglas may be proud to follow; lead on,
and I shall follow you!" He was shot
down a minute after, and the next who was
knocked over was your good-man, Mrs.
Garth—poor John! Ah! my niece,' he
interrupted himself, on seeing the suddenly arrested gaze of their guest. 'Mr.
Falconer of "Ours," Mary—Miss Montgomerie.'

Mary gave him her hand and a smile of welcome, and was at once put at her ease, as Sir Piers resumed his anecdote, to which, though she had heard it a hundred times before, Mrs. Garth listened with rapt attention, as became an 'old campaigner,' while Annabelle Erroll, who seemed already to have discovered that she and Mr. Falconer had some friend or friends in common, was conversing away with more than her usual fluency and animation.

'Is she already smitten by our new sub?' thought Mary.

Falconer had certainly a striking face and striking figure, and both were well calculated to please a woman's eye. In plain but accurate evening costume, the funereal costume of festive civilisation, he seemed every inch a gentleman and a handsome fellow; calm, self-possessed, and in about his twenty-fifth year; soldier-like, perfectly well-bred, as it eventually proved, was well-read and a skilful musician.

His nose was somewhat aquiline; his eyes and close-shaven hair were, like

Mary's, of the darkest brown, and his moustaches, as Annabelle afterwards whispered to her, were 'the perfection' of such appendages. He had a placid and perfectly assured manner, very different from Hew's alternate restlessness and *insouciance;* yet his eyes bespoke a latent fire of character and a spirit that was full of courage and energy ; and now Hew, who had been preparing for the coming meal by having either sherry and bitters, or a hideous compound called a 'cocktail,' which he had taught the butler, Tunley, to make up, came lounging in, with scrutiny and gloom in his eyes, to complete the little circle grouped near the fire.

By nature suspicious and envious, he barely accorded their visitor a touch of his hand, and from that moment these two young men felt—they knew not why—an instinctive dislike of each other.

The dinner-gong cut short another anecdote of the general's, and recalled his thoughts from pig-sticking and Central India ; he gave, with courtly old-fashioned politeness, his arm to Mrs. Garth; Mary took that of Cecil Falconer, and smiling Annabelle Erroll fell to the lot of the amiable Hew, while Mr. Tunley and the servants drew up rank entire in the vestibule; then, of course, the meal that followed was like any other in such an establishment, perfect, from the soup and dry sherry to the coffee and Maraschino.

'Tunley,' said Sir Piers, 'fill Mr. Falconer's glass. Glad to welcome you to Eaglescraig,' he added, bowing over a brimming glass of sherry; 'glad, indeed, to welcome one of my old Cameronians. I hope that, like me, you are proud of the old corps?'

'I am indeed, Sir Piers!' responded the young fellow with a kindling eye, that doubtless, like his heart, brightened under the genial and charming influences of his surroundings. 'I share, sir, to the full, the opinion of someone who says that no soldier is worth his salt unless he feels that he is as good as any man about him, and twice as good as any opposed to him.'

'Bravo, Falconer! you are one after my own heart! Gad, but he is a fine fellow,' he added in a low voice to Mrs. Garth; 'reminds me powerfully of some one I knew, long ago. *Who* the deuce can it be?'

In the extremity of his kindness at that moment, he actually thought him like his dead son, so the old man's whole heart went out to the new-comer, in whose favour this fanciful idea operated powerfully. 'His father and mother have long been dead, I understand, and he joined the Cameronians fresh from school—a mere boy, as I did myself.'

He looked almost tenderly on the young man, who was quite unconscious that he was an object of any particular interest; and his eyes kindled, but a sigh escaped as he recalled his own hot youth, and

'Thought of the days that were long since gone by,
  When his limbs were strong and his courage was
      high,'

and ere his once firm and stately stride had given place to what he called 'a species of half-pay shamble.'

'By the way, Falconer,' said Sir Piers,
whose pet weakness was pedigree, 'there
was an old family of your name, who had
an estate in this Bailiwick of Cunninghame
—perhaps you are a branch of it?'

The young man coloured rather perceptibly (as Hew was not slow to perceive and
make a note of), and said with a smile:

'I was educated out of Scotland; my
father died in my youth, and my mother
set no store on such fortuitous things as
name or pedigree.'

'A sad mistake,' said Sir Piers, shaking
his white head. 'The Falconers I speak
of were a branch of the Falconers, lords of
Halkertoun, who took their name from
their office, being falconers to our kings of
old, as we learn from Douglas—aye, so far
back as the twelfth century.'

'I know not, general, of what Falconers
I come,' replied the young officer a little
curtly; then he added, with a smile: 'I
only know that I was not born with the
proverbial silver spoon, but with a wooden
one, of the largest size.'

Sir Piers felt intuitively that he had touched a delicate subject, and changed it at once, though for a Scotsman not to know what kith or kin he came of seemed certainly incomprehensible; but Hew, aware of the vast value he attached to the most fortuitous circumstances of birth, family, and position, thought:

'No pedigree! By Jove! our Cameronian will find but small favour here now.'

'Tunley has got some magnificent Marcobruner and Lafitte in the cellar, Falconer,' said Sir Piers; 'I must have your opinion—but if I only look at them, I should have a twinge of my old enemy the gout.'

Falconer bowed his thanks, and was turning again to address Mary, when Sir Piers took his attention by plunging once more into Central India, and a stream of anecdotes about 'what the service and the regiment were in *my* time,' till the ladies withdrew, and, to Hew's disgust, there followed, of course, a professional conversation, on which he was totally unable to enter;

thus he could only sip his wine, toy with
the grape-scissors, or crack an occasional
nut, while hearing Sir Piers laughing at
jokes that seemed destitute of all fun to
him, and all matters of ' shop ' were discussed with the keenest relish—the new
head-dress for the Line, the new pattern
musket, and endless anecdotes of the mess-
room and parade, to all of which Hew, not
unnaturally, perhaps, listened with ill-dis-
guised impatience ; and even when the
conversation halted irregularly between
music and literature, or art and politics,
home and foreign, he could not enter
thereon, as Hew abhorred all books save a
betting one, and read no journal save the
Sporting Times.

Cecil Falconer rose to rejoin the ladies,
but the general was in no mood to spare
him, and insisted again and again on one
more glass of dry sherry, ' just as a white-
washer ;' and of course that, ' by the way,'
reminded him of ' how we used to be
annoyed at Agra by the musk-rats running
over the wine-bottles, and communicating

a confounded flavour of musk to the sherry, which is no improvement to the wine, I can tell you; and it is a curious fact that every English resident in India tastes musk in his wine at some time or other, though there are some who assert it is a mere superstition. When we were at Agra and elsewhere up country, we had deuced little money among us in the Cameronians, yet somehow we always spent a devil of a lot of it; for every fellow drew a bill on every other fellow, so there was a regular cross-fire of blue paper from right to left.'

To these and other reminiscences Falconer listened with his mind full of the bright smile accorded to him by Mary Montgomerie, when he had adroitly anticipated Hew in opening the door when the ladies departed to the drawing-room, whither he longed to follow them, and from whence the notes of the piano seemed to come as an invitation to do so, but he was compelled to endure anecdotes about India *ad nauseam.*

'By Jove, Sir Piers,' said Hew, wearily,

'I detest India; I've had enough of
it !'

'I don't mean you to have any more of
it, Hew, and you know that well,' replied
Sir Piers kindly, his heart mellowed with
wine ; ' but you are mistaken in your views
of it. " India," says a writer, correctly, I
think, " is quite a misrepresented country,
and has nothing objectionable in it, but a
tiger or two, and a little heat in the warm
part of the day." '

The night was considerably advanced
when they joined the ladies. Mrs. Garth
had already retired ; and the jolly old
general, who had fully partaken of more
wine than he usually did, stood in orderly-
room fashion, with his feet apart on the
rich hearthrug and his back to the fire,
winking, blinking, smiling blandly, and not
sure whether he was expected to take the
field at the head of the Cameronians to-
morrow ; while at the piano there was per-
formed a little brilliant singing, which Hew,
with growing irritation, secretly stigmatised
as ' the most duffing caterwauling !' and sat

apart sulking (wine had usually this effect
upon him), and leaving to Falconer the inevitable and pleasant task of turning the
music leaves, and his eyes watched alternately the handsome and well-formed young
fellow, who bent with ease and confidence
admiringly over the singers, who, with
voices sweetly attuned, were performing a
duet, and the forms of the latter, so different in the character of their beauty—
Mary with her hair of rich dark brown,
and Annabelle, the blonde, with her sunny
coils, that shone with a remarkable sheen
in the flood of radiance that fell from the
chandelier.

But the night waned apace, and at last
it was necessary to separate, if any justice
was to be done to the cover shooting on
the morrow, now close at hand.

Hew gave Falconer his hand, which to
the latter seemed clammy and quite like
the tail of a fish; but the general insisted
on escorting him to his 'quarters,' as he
said, and conducted him, candle in hand,
along one or two stately corridors adorned

with fine paintings—two, that were of Cardinal York and King James VIII., evinced the Jacobite proclivities of Sir Piers' ancestors—and there, too, were trophies of the chase, both European and Asiatic. Never had Hew or the girls known the usually grave and rather stately old baronet 'in such a merry pin' (Hew suggested 'so screwed'); but as he threaded the corridors he was heard to sing a scrap of an old Anglo-Indian ditty:

'Good-bye to the *batta !*—to lighten
    The pangs of each blooming cadet;
And the brows of the captains to brighten,
    They've doubled the one epaulette;
They've added some lace to our jackets,
    Augmented the price of our caps,
In the hope that the half-batta rackets
    Will merge in the glare of our "traps."
Just as any new plaything bewitches
    The sulks out of little boys whipped;
And before they've well pulled up their breeches,
    They wholly forget they've been stripped.'

'Ah, yes, Falconer, my lad, that song was known long before your day, when the beggars cut down the *batta.* But here you are—no, here; this is the door. Good-

night; hope you'll sleep sound. No need
for a chowree to whisk inside the curtains
here, as in India, and after making them safe
all round the mattress, spring in through
the hole you leave (like Harlequin through
his hoop), lest a cloud of mosquitoes follow.
I remember, at Dumdum—no, at Dina-
pore, my son Piers and Ballachulish of
the Cameronians——' Then his voice broke
as he spoke of his son, and he added : 'But
I'll tell you about it to-morrow. Breakfast
at nine, and then—hey for the covers !'

And now Sir Piers, whose voice had
become certainly somewhat 'feathery,' betook him to his own room, pausing on the
way more than once, candle in hand, as
his aristocratic ideas of family, and that
pride of birth which had been his ruling
passion and sin in early life, occurred to
him, and he muttered, pausing in his progress to bed, and shaking his white head :

'Doesn't know what Falconers he's of—
a strange thing—a pity. My boy Piers forgot, too, what Montgomeries *he* was of,
once on a time. A fine fellow, though !'

As for the latter, he was simply enchanted with Eaglescraig and all the details thereof: the beauty of the two girls, each so different in its character, and the *savoir vivre* of the old general. As for Hew, he forgot all about him.

Meanwhile, a few rooms distant, the lady's-maid was sleepily combing out the dark and luxuriant tresses of Mary Montgomerie, and the light of a shaded lamp fell softly and tenderly upon the graceful figures of herself and Annabelle, seated in their *robes de chambre* (chatting as young girls will always do when preparing for rest), on the looped-up lace curtains of their pretty beds, knotted one with blue and the other with rose-coloured ribbons; on the toilet-tables, with their glittering trinkets, and crystal bottles with gold or silver stoppers; on vases of conservatory flowers, and all the pretty luxuries which are usually to be found in the vicinity of youth, wealth, and beauty, as each girl sat smilingly contemplating herself in a long looking-glass, with all her rippling hair floating down over her white shoulders.

'And you like him?' said Mary, after the maid had withdrawn.

'Oh, so much!' exclaimed Annabelle; 'he is quite a dear fellow.'

'He has a gentle voice and gentle eyes, certainly,' said Mary, musingly.

'And to me looks somehow like one who has a history beyond that of other young men.'

'A history—what a funny idea! Of course he'll have a history, which, perhaps, like other young subs, he would rather not have made patent to everyone. But you and he seemed to have some little interest in common, Annabelle?'

'Had we?' said the latter, colouring a little.

'He spoke to you often of his friend, the other sub—what is his name?'

'Leslie Fotheringhame,' replied Annabelle in a low voice.

'Do you wish Sir Piers had invited *him?*'

'Perhaps, Mary,' said Annabelle, with a little forced laugh. 'Yet better not, better not,' she thought, with a memory of the days when her hand had thrilled at the touch of Leslie's, even before words of love had been spoken, and there had only been in her ear those broken utterances which a woman seldom, perhaps never, forgets.

So, save in the instance of Hew, all their first impressions of each other were favourable, and the young girls, as each laid her head on her pillow, began already to scheme out pleasant little visions, they scarcely knew of what.

CHAPTER IV.

COVER SHOOTING.

JOVIAL and laughing was the party which assembled at breakfast next day, in the bright morning-room of Eaglescraig, though the December landscape looked bleak enough without.

Mary, in all the freshness of her morning beauty, presided at one end of the loaded table, and Mrs. Garth at the other. Sir Piers was still in his room; but there was Cecil Falconer, in a shooting-suit of the best taste, and having of course innumerable pockets; Hew in rather 'loud'-patterned knickerbockers; a couple of jolly, red-faced country gentlemen, the village doctor, and **old Mr. John Balderstone** (of whom much more anon), the trusted land agent and local factor of **Sir Piers**, and deemed one of the best shots in the Baili-wick of Cunninghame, a hale, hearty, ruddy-faced man, with an ample paunch and short sturdy legs encased in long brown gaiters.

'How is Sir Piers this morning, Mr. Hew?' he asked that personage, who was intent on a pile of grouse pie, for the breakfast was a genuine Scottish one, a veritable dinner, with the addition of tea and coffee pots covered with elaborate cosies of Mary's handiwork. 'Well, I hope, and that he goes to shoot with us?'

'Well?—I should think so; hearty and lively,' replied Hew, with his mouth full; ' by Jove, he looks as if he was likely to live for ever! He's got the receipt for old Parr's life pills, and the secret of Methuse-lah too,' was the ungenerous—even coarse —response of Hew, half spoken to himself, and speaking volumes as to his secret thoughts; a response which made worthy old John Balderstone first raise and then knit his shaggy grey eyebrows; ' but here he comes, to answer for himself.'

Laughing and smiling, he greeted all in rapid succession, Cecil Falconer perhaps first of all, and then he kissed Mary; and anyone who saw how old Sir Piers held her hand and gazed into her tender hazel eyes, might have seen and known that she was the one hope of his now childless old age, and I doubt if he would have dined or breakfasted comfortably without her.

He bowed over the hand of Annabelle Erroll, with something of stately, old-fashioned courtesy; he patted Hew on the head as if he had been a boy, and then took a place beside him, after a glance at the weather without, with reference to the shooting. He wore a suit of rough grey tweed, with strong shoes and long brown leather leggings, that had seen service many a time and oft among the beans and turnip-fields all round Eaglescraig; and yet in this—the plainest of all costumes—he looked every inch what he was, a grand-looking and aristocratic old gentleman.

Shooting anecdotes, the qualities of certain dogs, guns, cartridges, new shot-belts, and so forth, were being discussed on all sides, together with eggs, ham, cold pie and steaming coffee; amid all of which Cecil Falconer strove in vain, even by the offer of a chicken-bone, to win the favour of Mary's pet terrier Snarley, which he was disposed for her sake to view and approach tenderly; but in return her favourite showed a whole set of sharp white teeth, and retreating under his mistress's chair, snarled and repelled the least attempt at familiarity, even when she caught the little brute up in her arms and bestowed upon it kisses, which to Cecil's eye seemed a great waste of something very charming.

'My pet, my own pet!' she called it, Snarley the while eyeing Falconer as if he was his natural enemy or future rival.

'Hope you slept well, Falconer?' said Sir Piers.

'Thanks—like a veritable top,' replied Cecil.

'Right! a regular soldier should be able to sleep anywhere, and never be surprised on awakening in new quarters.'

'Been ever in this part of the world before, sir?' asked Mr. John Balderstone, with his mouth full.

'Never,' replied Cecil.

'Ah, you'll soon learn to like Eagles-craig,' added the factor.

'I am enchanted with it already,' said Cecil, as his eye involuntarily wandered in Mary's direction; 'and believe that I shall like it more and more, till it will be quite a wrench when the time comes to tear myself away.'

'Then come back, Falconer, for some rod-fishing after Candlemas,' suggested his host, with a bright smile.

'Duty, I fear, may clash with your great hospitality; but I thank you, Sir Piers.'

'Call me general; I like it better.'

'To be always called so is my uncle's pet fancy, Mr. Falconer,' said Mary.

'All great men have their weaknesses, and I always respect them,' remarked Hew, with one of his scarcely perceptible sneers, for now Sir Piers, to his irritation, had plunged into some reminiscences of snipe-shooting at Dumdum, where he was wont to be for some hours up to the waist in water under a burning Bengal sun, necessitating frequent libations of brandy-pawnee; then, by some rapid transition of thought, he found himself detailing a march of the Cameronians through the jungles of Arcot, with the rain pouring in torrents, the road knee-deep in mud and mire, the men drenched, the tents soaked through, the mess and baggage animals miles in the rear, the column having to cross a nullah where the water ran like a mill-race, and there was the devil to pay!

Other anecdotes would have followed, but Hew, who had seen enough of India in reality too, proposed a move to the gun-room and thence to the covers.

'Time indeed to be off, gentlemen,' said

the general, looking at his watch. ' Tunley, fill those flasks.'

' And have more sandwiches cut,' added Mrs. Garth.

' I shall cut them for Mr. Falconer ; he is the only stranger here,' said Mary Montgomerie, hurrying to the sideboard, and proceeding deftly with her pretty hands to do so ; while Cecil murmured his thanks, and tendered his silver case, or sandwich-box.

' Can't the cook do this ?' growled Hew in her ear.

' Yes, but not half so well as I,' replied the girl, laughingly. ' I can be so expert when I choose, Hew.'

In the hall, where hung all manner of hats and greatcoats, plaids, whips, salmon-listers, whips and walking-sticks, Sir Piers assumed an old and well-worn wideawake, the band of which was usually garnished with hooks and flies, for he was as keen a sportsman with his rod and line as with his double-barrelled gun. And now the whole party set forth from the house,

Cecil looking more than once to the soft faces of the two smiling girls, who, from the breakfast-room window, watched their departure.

His mind *already* was full of sweet Mary Montgomerie, and he would rather, a thousand times, have remained to sun himself in the light of her winning eyes, than to toil through the damp covers to knock over a few rabbits or a brace of harmless birds; and he could but console himself by counting the hours that must inevitably elapse ere he could meet her again, and strive to endure them as best he might.

Hew detected one of these glances thrown back to ' the face at the window,' and remembering his ramble with Mary in the Dovecot Park, bit his nether lip ; and before the day's shooting was over, Falconer had a specimen of what the amiable Hew might be capable of doing if provoked.

Preoccupied thus, Cecil Falconer thought that on this particular morning ' the Land

of Burns' seemed uncommonly dreary.
Mist was rolling along the valleys, and the
landscape looked dank and moist through
its medium.

Hew, who, though not ungentlemanlike
in bearing, was, as we have said, naturally
coarse in mind, and sometimes blunt in
manner, the result of association with
billiard-markers and stablemen, on seeing
Falconer give another glance towards the
house, said abruptly, and with what he
meant to be a laugh :

' I don't think you can see her now.'

' Her—who ?' asked Falconer, with surprise.

'Well, my cousin ; for I think you
evidently admire her.'

' An odd remark !' thought Cecil, looking
a little annoyed ; but he said, cordially :

' I do indeed admire her ; who could
fail to do so ? But what leads you to infer
that I do so more particularly ?'

' By Jove ! I saw that your eyes were
seldom off her ; but it is no use, Mr.
Falconer,' said Hew, with a pretended

genial laugh, 'as she has no eyes in reality—save for one fellow.'

' *What* the deuce can he mean ?' thought Falconer, a little annoyed by the speaker's manner, which seemed to indicate advice or warning, or impertinence.

'You are cousins, then ?' he merely said coldly.

'Well, of course, in a manner of way—rather remote, you know,' replied Hew, his closely-set eyes looking more shifty than ever, as he scraped a match and lighted a huge cigar ; 'but blood is thicker than water, and it goes a long way in Scotch reckonings ; and thus she naturally looks to *me* as the future head of the house,' he added complacently, 'as the heir of entail. And Mary is indeed handsome ! There was no girl handsomer out last season, or when she was presented —I mean in the quiet and thoroughbred style.'

' What a cad this fellow is !' thought Falconer.

' Ah, you have looked admiringly back

at the house,' said Sir Piers, who had another theory on the subject; 'the old tower is the part of it that is most to my taste. The cliff was called Eaglescraig, because ages ago a couple of gigantic eagles built a nest there every summer— a nest of branches and great sticks on the giddy verge of the cliff—and the vicinity of it was always found strewed with the bones of muirfowl, ptarmigan, rabbits, and even lambs. A poor man who lived near it made quite a subsistence for himself and his family, during a famine consequent on an English invasion, by robbing the eaglets of the food brought by the parents; and one day he found a little fair-skinned and golden-haired child therein, brought no one knew from where, by the male bird, but safe and sound. It grew to be a man of vast strength and stature, and he carried the banner of the Bailiwick at the battle of Largs—and certainly that field was not fought and won yesterday.'

The day was unquestionably a bleak one. The last few leaves were fluttering

down from the bare trees, the branches and
twigs of which stood blankly and darkly
up against the dull grey sky; elsewhere
the red and brown remnant of rustling
foliage that still lingered on the oaks and
ashes was thinned by every passing breeze;
and even the gay cock pheasant, as he
skimmed over the gorse to seek his food
in the untilled land, might be heard to
croak as he went.

Grim old Sandy Swanshot, the head-
keeper, and his staff, had already traversed
the covers; the muzzled ferrets had been
down in the rabbit burrows, scaring forth
the occupants; firm, stealthy, and quick-
eyed, they drove them into the gorse or
elsewhere, and now the earth had been
stopped everywhere, barring all return to
their well-known holes, which they would
never find again.

The cottage of the keeper, old Sandy,
a veteran sportsman, silver-haired and
wrinkled, who had often carried the
general's game-bag when they were both
'school laddies,' was a busy scene that

morning. It was a thatched edifice, gar-
landed round with dead wild-cats, weasels,
foumarts, hawks, and ' other vermin,' which
in their decay tainted the winter air, and
its occupant was old enough to remember
when the system of shooting with muzzle-
loaders was very different from what it is
to-day; when a cover was beaten with a
precision quite military, and when the
order ' Halt ! reload !' went down the line,
every man, be he shooter or beater, had
to stop where he was, until the last barrel
had been charged anew; and the old man
had a supreme contempt for the perilous
style of blazing away that had come in with
arms of precision and the slaughter of
battues.

All the dogs around him seemed to
know instinctively that they were about to
take the field, and kept up a chorus of
mingled whining and barking; and all the
beaters were there, somewhat motley in
aspect and appearance, but all doffing their
bonnets respectfully, as Sir Piers came up
with his ' guns ' from the manor-house;

and each of the latter underwent, unknown to himself, a critical scrutiny under
the keen eyes of these practised fellows—
his dress, his gun, his gaiters, his shot-
belt, every buckle and strap being duly
noticed and commented on.

We may hope that Cecil Falconer's bearing and equipment carried him through this
unknown ordeal; but the old keeper, who
had an instinctive dislike of Hew Montgomerie, whispered to him as a stranger,
though Sandy was, in Scottish parlance, a
dour carl :

'Gie him a wide berth in the cover,
sir! Shooting? *he* might as well be bal-
looning!'

Sandy knew some of Hew's vagaries
when at cover, such as shooting down the
line of the beaters and his companions,
letting fly at a bird whose flight was no
higher than a man's head, fingering his
trigger, heedless of whether the muzzle
was pointed to the sky or the earth, and
as careless of his friends as if they were
clad in Milan mail; for he was one of

those awkward fellows who had not even the simple prudence which Charles Dickens ascribes to the obese Mr. Tracy Tupman, when that personage discovered that his chief object was to fire his gun without danger to his friends, himself, or the dogs.

The covers of Eaglescraig were of considerable extent, and were well preserved and carefully looked after; and though Sir Piers, as he said, thought it very slow work compared with pig-sticking in six-foot-high jungle-grass, or potting a man-eater from a howdah, it was what suited him now, and in less than five minutes he had all his 'guns' in 'order of battle,' marshalled apart in a line of about a hundred and forty yards or so, the beaters being chequered in the gaps between the sportsmen.

Advancing thus, like skirmishers in extended order, on the right flank of the line, were masses of whin-bush (or gorse as it is called in England), displaying still here and there a golden flower; and away on the left the cover went deep into the dark recesses of a copse, under the tall red stems of Scottish firs, larch, and ash-trees.

Hew and Cecil were in this quarter, and a little in the rear was the keeper, the latter scanning the whole, as far as he well could, from flank to flank, rebuking from time to time, in his deep, broad Ayrshire Doric, any stupid beater who lagged behind, while the sharp crack of the guns woke the echoes of the dingles, which occasionally seemed to reply to quite an irregular volley.

Among the gorse the chief victims were ground game, but amid the coppice the ruddy golden-hued pheasants were momentarily flurried up, and arrested in their whirring flight by the crack of the fatal breechloader.

Ever and anon, the voice of the keeper was heard, with the prohibitory cry of—

''Ware hen—'ware hen, Master Hew!'

Among much other spoil, Cecil knocked over a fine cock-pheasant, which fell crash-

ing down among the underwood in the
agonies of death—a charge of shot in his
gold-speckled breast.

'Why the deuce did you shoot my bird,
sir?' demanded Hew with uncourteous abruptness of Falconer.

'He thocht, perhaps, ye war gaun to
miss it, as ye did the last twa, and the
hare,' said the old keeper, drily.

'I beg your pardon,' replied Cecil quietly,
as he reloaded; 'but that bird was mine.'

'It was *not!*' was the blunt and rude
rejoinder.

Falconer coloured and bit his lip; but
thought of his courtly old host, and desirous of avoiding a scene, simply said:

'Let us keep further apart, Mr. Montgomerie.'

'As far off as you please,' added Hew
ungraciously, and moving further away to
his left.

Cecil continued to work his way between
the crowded fir and larch stems, which, by
receiving many a charge of shot, saved the
birds that hovered beyond them, the voice

of the keeper crying ever and anon :
' Mark cock !' ' Hare forward !' ' 'Ware
hen.' ' A hare for you, Master Hew—a
miss again !' ' Come to heel, Countess—
come to heel !' the latter, with the vicious
whack of a whip, was directed to one of the
pointers.

While Cecil was inwardly laughing at
Hew's wild shooting, a charge of shot from
the right whizzed past his face and tore
away the rim of his hat.

A natural exclamation of rage and alarm
escaped him, as he had so narrowly escaped
having his sight destroyed or his face dis-
figured for life, and looking whence the shot
came, he saw Hew gently slipping another
cartridge into the breech of his gun, under
cover of a great Scottish fir with a red
gnarled stem.

' I shall thank you, sir, to keep your
muzzle up, or quit the ground !' said Falconer, angrily.

' It was a devil of a mistake—and I beg
your pardon,' replied Hew, giving his cold
damp hand to Cecil, who saw—or thought

he saw—a quiet twinkle of mingled malice
and amusement in the speaker's bilious
eye.

'Blundering fool! Could he have meant
it?   Looks deuced like it—but why?'
thought the young officer more angrily,
as he thought over the matter.

'He weel-nigh shot Sir Piers in the
same unco fashion, sir,' grumbled the
old keeper; while Cecil now changed his
ground again, and for actual safety kept
closer to Hew than ever.

Four long beats through the covers
brought luncheon-time, and while flasks
and sandwiches were produced, the slain
were counted as they were laid in long
rows on the side of a grassy bank, each
keeper, as he came up in succession, adding
his quota to the general stock, all furred
and feathered victims from the covers of
Eaglescraig, and so numerous, that the
sportsmen thought enough had been done
for one day.

'I may deem myself lucky that I was
not added to *your* bag to-day, Mr. Mont-

gomerie,' said Cecil, laughing, but not with genuine hilarity.

'What! has Hew been at his old tricks again?' asked Sir Piers, with an air of annoyance.

'E'en sae, sir,' said Sandy, taking a flask from his mouth, 'firing doon the line as before.'

'My gun exploded unexpectedly, sir,' said Hugh, with a sullen look; 'I explained to Mr. Falconer, and he has accepted my apology.'

Something in his manner caused this episode to rankle in the memory of Cecil.

'By Jove, I think the cad *had* intended to pot me, after all!' was his occasional thought, and he never precisely forgot or forgave the suspicion—one too grave in its diabolical spirit of mischief and cruelty to be dismissed lightly; and though he laughed at some jokes made by old Mr. Balderstone on the matter, he really saw nothing to laugh at in it, and was very well pleased when the whole party bent their steps homeward—all the more pleased when he thought of the pleasant society that awaited him.

Falconer began to wonder whether he was actually falling in love already with the beautiful grand-niece of his host. He had never believed much in 'that sort of thing,' at first sight especially; but he was young and impressionable; he possessed a keen imagination, and he already caught himself weaving mental conversations with her—conversations in which tender little speeches came involuntarily, though unuttered, to his lips, and soft smiles hovered on hers, when she seemed to hear them; but when—after changing his muddy shooting-costume for another—he joined the ladies in the drawing-room, remembering the almost rude remarks of Hew Montgomerie, Cecil, in approaching Mary, or conversing with her, had an angry sense of being watched, or observed, by that personage; though a time came when he ceased to think or care on the subject.

And *who* was 'the one fellow' for whom she had only eyes, as Hew had vulgarly phrased it? Most probably Hew meant himself! If so, Cecil thought that she cloaked or concealed her partiality with wonderful discretion.

To avoid interfering with that gentleman's views or wishes, Cecil gave much of his attention to Annabelle Erroll, and even to 'the old soldier,' as Hew called Mrs. Garth ; but Mary summoned him to her side to see Snarley put through all his performances, such as leaping over her interlaced hands as through a ring, walking erect round the room for a lump of sugar, tossing another high off his sharp nose at the word of command, to catch it with a snap in its descent, and so forth, all the while he did so eyeing Cecil with undisguised hostility.

And eventually the evening closed in like the preceding one (save that old Sir Piers, worn out with his day's sport, had fallen asleep in an easy-chair, with a handkerchief spread over his face), with music and duet-singing, and pleasant conversation, ere some of the visitors rose to depart.

That there should be so much duet-singing, and Mary's occupation with the stranger, and that the general conversation was of a kind in which he could bear no prominent part, disgusted Hew, who was in a detestable humour ; yet he had the policy to conceal it pretty well (though his bilious eye was more bilious than ever) till once, he drew near Mary, while Cecil, in another part of the room, was occupied with old Mrs. Garth, who was relating with great unction some memory of the Cameronians in *her* day ; and now Hew's ready jealousy became painfully apparent.

'Good heavens, Hew !' said Mary, in a low voice, her dark eyes dilating as she spoke ; ' what is this Mr. Balderstone has told us ?'

'Can't say, for the life of me ; the old pump !'

'That you nearly shot Mr. Falconer to-day in the Fir Wood.'

'Did I ? Well, the blundering fellow was out of his proper place, I suppose,' was the sulky rejoinder.

'What a dreadful thing if you had injured him!' Hew! you are positively dangerous.'

'My dear Mary, you deem him an Admirable Crichton, I doubt not,' said he, smilingly, in her ear.

'What do *you* deem him?'

'Slow and deuced ugly.'

'Ugly—oh, come, Hew!' said Mary, laughing very merrily at such undisguised jealousy, which somehow did not flatter her in the least—it was too comical.

'I have no doubt our "old soldier" here deems him a very eligible *parti* for anyone; a subaltern, with two shirts a week and a few dickies, by Jove!' he continued.

'How—how coarse you are!' said Mary, with her silvery laugh again; 'but don't let grand-uncle hear you sneering thus. He, too, was a subaltern once.'

'Yes, but with the rent-roll of Eaglescraig! I wish him well out of our neighbourhood anyway,' he added threateningly.

'Why, what harm has he done you?'

'None as yet,' replied Hew, getting

more sulky than ever ; 'but I may harm him !'

'How ?'

'If he comes in my way with you, Mary, or anyone else—understand that clearly, cousin.'

Mary's brow darkened, and a haughty expression, not unmixed with alarm, stole into her hazel eyes and soft face, as she said, while quickly using her fan :

'Hew, you forget yourself, and me too ! How dare you adopt this tone ?'

'Don't think to make a fool of me, Mary.'

'Impossible, sir !'

'You think so ?'

'Yes. Nature has been before me,' she replied, as she rose and swept across the room to the side of old Mr. Balderstone.

The eyes of Hew, like those of Uriah Heep, 'seemed to take any shade of colour that could make eyes ugly,' as they followed her beautiful figure, and a savage emotion gathered in his avaricious heart as he felt that the chances of his wooing

with success—a wooing that was without
pure love—were receding further away
than ever ; but whatever were his thoughts,
to show that there was no bad feeling
between Cecil Falconer and himself, after
all had retired to rest that night, he invited the former to have a quiet little
game of écarté in the smoking-room—a
game from which the Cameronion did *not*,
somehow, come away a winner.

CHAPTER V.

HEW MAKES A VOW.

OR the next few days Cecil Falconer continued to give Hew a 'grey wide berth,' as the old keeper phrased it, at the covers, where each day's shooting was precisely like that which preceded it. If Hew, thought Falconer, were capable of such mad jealousy and dastardly cruelty after a few hours' acquaintance, of what might he not be capable and guilty in the time to come?

Was it his blundering stupidity which, as the gamekeeper said, had nearly cost Sir Piers his life once before, or a spirit of infernal malevolence to revenge the petty dispute about the cock-pheasant, that made him fire his gun in the way he had done ?

At times Cecil was inclined to give him the benefit of the doubt, and as he was not of a resentful temperament, he gradually either forgot the event, or remembered it only as a mistake, that might have proved more serious than it did. So each day's shooting passed pleasantly over, and the evenings were devoted to music in the drawing-room, where Mrs. Garth dispensed tea at a pretty little oval table—fragrant orange Pekoe, out of tiny eggshell cups, without handles—and where Sir Piers fell fast asleep over his *Scotsman;* and the night wound up by Hew luring Falconer into what he termed ' a little mild play ' in the smoking-room—play from which the latter always rose a loser, without being able precisely to know how.

Save for this kind of thing, which he could ill afford, Falconer thought the brief term of his leave would be delightfully spent at Eaglescraig. A ' green yule ' had come and gone, without skating or

curling, and the owl whooped nightly on
the old tower-head, where the winter wind
shook the masses of ivy on the time-worn
walls; and the New Year was ushered in
with well-bred joviality, rather than the
hearty old-fashioned uproariousness of the
olden time, though in the drawing-room
the chorus could be heard from the servant's hall, where Mr. Tunley led it with
joyous vociferation, singing,

'Here's a health to the year that's awa'!'

And precisely as the house-clocks struck
twelve—midnight—the house-door was un-
barred with great formality, and thrown
open to let the Old Year *out*, and the
New Year *in;* and rising from his elbow-
chair, Sir Piers kissed his niece Mary, and
then old Mrs. Garth in a courtly fashion,
an example Hew Montgomerie was not
slow to follow on the soft cheek of the
former, while Falconer looked laughingly,
yet perhaps enviously, on, and dared only
press her hand as he did that of Miss
Erroll; and then there was a general hand-

shaking with Mr. Balderstone and other
old friends who had been invited to join
the social circle.

The rubicund Mr. Tunley offered, in the
name of all the servants, to drink their
old master's good health, and the health of
all the family ; and Sir Piers, natheless
all his pride, cordially shook the old
butler's hand, and each wished the other
many happy years to come ; and he went
through the same ceremony with all in the
servants' hall.

In all this homely warmth, mutual
kindness and goodwill, there was much
that charmed Falconer; for though be-
longing to a Scottish regiment, and one
famous in history, educated as he had
been far away from his native country,
and under peculiar circumstances, he knew
little or nothing of the ways and customs
of the latter.

He had been much a wanderer, and never
knew a home, save such as he had found
with his regiment ; so there was much
in the little circle at Eaglescraig to delight

him. Save with Hew, he won golden opinions from all there ; his genial manner, spirited good-humour, handsome bearing, and facile mode of adapting himself to those among whom chance threw him—a mode that came, perhaps, of his having been educated abroad—all seemed to make him a prime favourite.

He could speak much, and pleasantly, of what he had seen and where he had been ; he was a reader, too, and the fruit of his reading cropped up pleasantly from time to time in the course of conversations that Hew could take little or no part in, greatly to his own wrath.

'What a place this is for gammon and spinach !' thought Hew, who viewed all this with extreme distaste, and still more the intimacy that progressed between this 'interloper,' as he deemed him, and Mary Montgomerie ; for they nightly played together the mazurkas of Chopin and selections from the songs of Mendelssohn and the operas of Verdi, while Hew looked darkly and dubiously on, thinking there

was in all this far more than met the eye;
and Sir Piers thought, with a smile, that a
Cameronian of *his* time would certainly not
have shone much as a pianist.

Mary was always so happy in herself,
that she usually made all others equally so;
thus, in her society, the hours, with
Falconer, seemed to fly like minutes.

Hew had—unknown to Sir Piers—become so seriously involved in monetary
matters during his sojourn in India, that it
was next to impossible for him to return
there; and his chief hope for retrieving
himself and doing well for the future lay
in a marriage with Mary Montgomerie,
rather than the prospective succession to
the baronetcy and to the acres of Eaglescraig, for Sir Piers was a hale old fellow
and might live for twenty years yet.
Indeed, everyone said so.

Thus he viewed with extreme bitterness
and jealousy the visit of Falconer and some
of the details attendant on that visit, and
his closely-set and parti-coloured eyes
twinkled dangerously as he muttered:

'Devil take me if I don't bowl that fellow out yet!'

If Hew had been tender and true, less brusque and coarse—had really loved Mary with a loving heart — she might have felt some compunction for her laughing indifference to his suit; but she knew well his avarice, his monetary hopes, and suspected some of his vices; and, more than all, her proud spirit revolted at the idea of being made by her father's will the mere puppet of a family compact, and *compelled* to marry any man.

'I heard you arranging a riding-party to-morrow, Mary,' said he, during a pause (or while Falconer was being accompanied in an Italian song by Miss Erroll), and bending over Mary till his moustache nearly touched the white and close division in her rich dark-brown hair, while she idled over an album of Indian photographs.

'Yes—you will go, of course, Hew?' said she, looking up at him with her sunny hazel eyes bright with a smile.

'I would rather be excused,' he replied, sulkily.

'Why?'

'Why? because I should be only in the way.'

'Please yourself, Hew; but I do not understand you,' said Mary, colouring with annoyance; '*what* do you mean?'

'I mean,' said he bluntly, and in a low, concentrated voice, 'that before this Cameronian fellow came, you and I were— were——'

'Were what?' asked Mary, sharply.

'Well, friends, at least.'

'And are we not friends now?' she said, laying her hand on his arm. He looked lingeringly at it—a lovely hand it was, round and white, with a golden bangle clasping the dimpled wrist—and he said in a low voice:

'I had hoped we should in time be something dearer——'

'Oh, stuff! Dear Hew, don't begin that sort of thing here,' replied Mary, laughing to conceal her annoyance; 'you will forget

all about it when you go back to India
again.'

Hew's face darkened ominously.

'But you don't like India?' added Mary,
somewhat teasingly, while a roguish smile
dimpled her cheeks.

'I hate it, as you know well; yet I may
have to return there, for all that you care
about it, or me.'

'There are tigers there, and snakes, and
all those sort of things, Hew?'

'Yes, and perhaps you would like them
to eat me?' he asked, viciously.

'Oh, Hew! how can you speak thus!'
she exclaimed, laughing. 'I never said
so.'

'But you thought it, all the same.'

She laughed louder at this, for Hew's
peculiar love-making, if it annoyed, always
excessively amused her at the same time—
a fatal element for him.

The morning of the proposed ride proved
a beautiful one, clear, bracing, and sunny,
and the horses were betimes brought round
from the stables to the stately perron in

front of the house, where Hew was smoking a cigar, when the girls came forth in their riding‑habits, attended by Cecil Falconer.

'And you are resolved not to accompany us, Hew?' asked Mary, coaxingly, desirous to please him.

'Yes,' he replied, bluntly.

'What a pity the season is not summer,' she said to Falconer, 'we could have such pleasant sketching expeditions, picnics, afternoon tea on the lawn, croquet‑matches and lawn‑tennis; but our picnics are so jolly, and we always use the big omnibus, in which the servants drive on Sundays to the kirk of Eaglescraig.'

'Croquet is only good for one thing,' muttered Hew; 'it enables a fellow to loaf with some girl he is soft upon; otherwise I never could see anything in it,' he added in his growling tone.

Slender and willowy looked the figure of Mary in her tight, well‑fitted habit, even more so than that of Miss Erroll, who was undoubtedly a very handsome girl.

Hew, having been in India, had been compelled to learn riding ; but he was a timid and indifferent cavalier, afraid of a horse, indeed, and he could never have done what he saw Mary doing, tickling, patting, and kissing the nose of her favourite pad, ere she was swung into her saddle so deftly by Cecil, to whose care and companionship, together with those of Annabelle Erroll, he was now compelled to relinquish her, as the three departed, merrily and laughingly, to visit the ruined castle of Kilbirnie, amid its stately parks and beautiful gardens.

Down the long avenue they went under oaks and elms that had been growing since the field of Pinkecleugh was fought and lost ; and between a pair of grand old carved iron gates, surmounted by a coat-of-arms and supported by massive stone pillars covered with grey lichen and green moss, and past the lodge, the occupant of which, an old wooden-legged Cameronian, stood at ' attention' as they issued out upon the roadway, watched by the evil eyes of

Hew, to begin a two hours' 'spin' through a rich and pastoral country.

Conversation of the stereotyped kind, concerning the weather and so forth, had been long ignored by Falconer and Miss Montgomerie.

'I shall show you some beautiful scenery,' said she, as they shortened their horses' pace to a walk; 'it is of the pastoral kind, of course—for this is the land of dairy-farms and Dunlop cheeses—all hill and dale; and though there are no mountains, we are very proud of Cunninghame,' she added, laughing. 'Do you draw?'

'Yes.'

'And paint?'

'A little, in water-colours.'

'What a pity it is winter-time! Were the season open, we might sketch together, and how delightful that would be!'

Cecil Falconer cordially agreed with her.

'You must know that I love all this place dearly, wood, wold, and water,' exclaimed the girl, with a bright smile, as she looked around her with eyes the greatest beauty of which was their happy expression, girlish truthfulness, and the innocence of a nature that had never sought either to simulate or conceal an emotion ; 'but I fear you will deem me very provincial.'

'Why—for loving your native place ?'

'Ah ! but this is *not* my native place. I was born far away from here ; but since poor papa followed mamma to her grave, I have lived at Eaglescraig, and all the happiest memories of my childhood, and girlhood too, are connected with it; so I love the bold rocky scenery, the great bluffs that overhang the Firth of Clyde, and the green pastoral valleys of Cunninghame. I know every farm and cottage, every coppice and wimpling burn, in the bailiwick.'

'Is it long since your parents died, Miss Montgomerie ?' asked Falconer, as their conversation began to take a personal turn.

'Yes ; oh, so long ago that I can only remember them as if in a dream !'

' That is sad.'

' And yours—was your father in the Cameronians ?'

' He died when I was in infancy ; and where, I scarcely know.'

' But he, too, was a soldier, of course ?'

' I think not,' said Falconer, evasively.

' I am too curious—pardon me ; but I am a terrible talker,' she added, and changed the subject, which Annabelle Erroll perceived had brought an unwonted colour to the young man's cheeks.

Falconer had often thought that, had his father lived, there would have been a great difference in his own life somehow, though he could not distinctly define the nature of it.

' How I wish your friend had been here with you,' Mary Montgomerie said, after a pause.

' Leslie Fotheringhame ?'

' Yes ; but Sir Piers said it was impossible.'

' He, too, could not leave our detachment.'

'How lonely he must be, shut up in that dull castle of Dumbarton. His name is a scarce one; is he one of the old Fotheringhames of Angus?'

'I believe so,' said Miss Erroll, colouring after she spoke.

'We should have made quite a pleasant quartette!' said Miss Montgomerie. 'Does he sing?'

'Oh yes—so well!' replied Annabelle, ere Falconer could speak.

'How do *you* know?' asked her friend, laughing.

Annabelle, usually taciturn and silent, now changed colour more perceptibly, and replied:

'Surely Mr. Falconer must have said so! How should *I* know, otherwise?'

Cecil was perfectly aware that he had never done so, but was puzzled to think how Miss Erroll was aware of his friend's talent.

'You have met, perhaps?' he began.

'In society—yes; people meet each other everywhere nowadays,' she replied, and looked another way.

The three riders were still in view of the loftily-situated house and tall old tower of Eaglescraig, and Hew's eyes, from the terrace, were following them.

He seemed still to see the skill and grace with which—as if he caressed her—Cecil Falconer had swung Mary Montgomerie into her saddle, and the care and tenderness with which he adjusted her stirrup, her habit, and reins. He seemed to see, too, the light in the eyes of both as they scampered down the long avenue, ere he turned away to get a foaming beaker of soda-and-brandy, in Mr. Tunley's pantry, as a panacea for his bitter thoughts.

He watched the trio disappear over a slope, or braehead, where the road dipped downward, and he registered a vow of vengeance on Cecil Falconer *if* the latter crossed his purposes—a vow all the deeper for being unspoken—and he achieved it terribly when the time came, and it was ultimately to assume a form and force beyond even what he himself could have conceived !

Nature had cursed Hew with a suspicious and jealous disposition ; inherent doubt of everyone was a part of that very disposition. Thus, his own total want of success with Mary Montgomerie, on one hand, led him, on the other, to conceive the most exaggerated ideas of the progress Cecil Falconer must already have made with her.

Hew Montgomerie, when he chose, could be 'a good hater,' and, as such, would have been decidedly after the heart of the 'great' English lexicographer, whose hateful addendum was, 'I never forgive an injury;' but Cecil had in no way injured Hew.

CHAPTER VI.

A REVELATION.

OF Cecil Falconer's mood of mind and views of the whole situation at this time, we can be best informed by a letter which he despatched to his friend and chum, Leslie Fotheringhame, on the day subsequent to the little riding expedition :

'Eaglescraig, Cunninghame.

'MY DEAR LESLIE,

'Hannibal has found his Capua ! After our limited *cuisine* at Dumbarton, it seems to me that—so far as luxury is concerned—daily Lucullus dines with Apicius ;

by which preamble you will think, old
fellow, that I have gone out of my mind, or
betaken me to cramming again, as we did
at Sandhurst.   I am freely quartered in a
magnificent house, with delightful society,
and an old host, the general, who is hospitality's own self, and possesses a well-filled
stable and a rare cellar—not that I care
for it much—but any way, in its binns are
some curious old Madeira that has been
thrice round the Cape, white and red Con-
stantia, Tokay with tints of gold, Chateau-
Yquem, and Malmsey in which maudlin
Clarence might have been drowned.

'We have had some excellent cover
shooting, and, though the birds were a little
wild, a good many brace fell to my bag.
Nothing is stiff or formal here, though the
old gentleman has some stately, eccentric,
and rather extravagant notions about
family, pedigree, blood, and all that sort of
thing, and laments much the loss of a son
who was once one of "Ours."   There are
two charming girls here, and after one's
bachelor and barrack experiences, it is de-

lightful to meet them each day at breakfast,
with their fresh morning costumes and
complexions ; and charming, too, is the
morning-room—quite like that described in
"Coningsby": " Such a profusion of flowers ;
such a multitude of books ; such a prodi-
gality of writing materials ; so many easy-
chairs too, of so many shapes, each in itself
a comfortable home ; yet nothing crowded."
And then the girls ! Don't you envy me,
old fellow ? But I have no doubt they
will have you over here when I—alas !—
leave, for the old double Dun in the Clyde.

'There is one blot in my picture—a
member of the family circle, named Hew
Caddish Montgomerie, to whom I am
obliged to do the civil, the general's heir—
whom I simply detest and view in the
light of a noxious reptile, why or how I
cannot precisely say ; but we have our
likings and dislikings in this world, our
attractions and repulsions, and *certes*, this
fellow repels me !

'He is jowly in face, with full, red lips,
heavy, stealthy, and shifty eyes, set close

to his nose, and he inherits rather reddish
hair and freckles from the family who
gave him his middle name, which, curiously
enough, is Caddish ; and in spite, jealousy,
or by a blunder, he nearly potted me one
day in the covers !

'I think he already views me as a species
of rival ; he is a sort of cousin of Miss
Montgomerie (would that I were so ! but I
am only one of those poor devils who exist
in the world on sufferance), and whether
they are engaged or not I cannot tell. He
has half led me to infer as much, and
assumes a disgusting air of proprietary and
so forth, which certainly is not endorsed by
Miss Montgomerie.'

(Falconer had written ' by *Mary*,' but
had dashed through the Christian name,
which had escaped his pen, and Fotheringhame remarked this.)

' Anyhow, I was cognisant of a rather
tender scene between them in the avenue
on the day I arrived here. He is deuced
sharp at cards, and I have already lost to
him much more than I can afford to lose.

'The general is an enthusiast on all that
pertains to the regiment, and quite a detachment of it, in the shape of old pensioners,
is quartered on his property. His Indian
anecdotes *are* a little prosy, as he lugs
them in on every conceivable occasion ; but
he is such a dear old fellow, that one can't
help listening to his yarns about curry and
rice ; and a curious one he told me, last
night, may interest you, as it referred to
his son and a detachment of " Ours."

' When they were in Central India, Piers
Montgomerie, with forty Cameronians and
some natives, invested a fort named the
Ghurry of Kittoor, a square edifice with
towers at the corners, armed with heavy
gingals and a few small cannon. The Potail
commanding it was a resolute fellow, be-
lieving himself shot-proof, by an amulet he
wore, and he was custodian of a great
amount of treasure in gold mohurs, of
which Piers had orders to deprive him.
The fort was stormed, the Potail slain, and
the treasure-chest was found, but totally
empty—verifying the last words of the

Potail, who, when dying, swore upon the Koran that there was not even an anna in the place, and that all the slaughter had been for nothing.

'Before the gate of the Ghurry there grew a tree of vast size and age, which Captain Montgomerie ordered his men to cut down for fuel. The soldier who hewed down the first branch brought away with it a literal shower of gold—gold that flashed in the sunshine and studded all the green sward like yellow buttercups; and there, sure enough, in the hollow trunk of the tree, was found treasure to the value of fifty thousand golden mohurs, to the bewilderment and joy of the Cameronians, who had been on such short rations for some time past, that they were ready to share the repast of Count Ugolino.

'I listen patiently to such yarns, because I am anxious to remain in his good graces; would that I could also be in those of his ward and niece !

'I believe, Leslie, that you are nearer to my heart than any other friend I ever had,

so I don't mind owning to you that I am in
for it—about to fall in love! I have
always been at the same old game, you
will say; but this time I fear that I am in
terrible earnest, and have met my fate!
But the deuce is, that she is a great heiress,
while I have only my pay, or little more,
and dare not lift my eyes so high; besides,
what would be the use, as I strongly suspect that, with the general's wish and
consent, she is the *fiancée* of his heir—the
most unamiable, yet enviable, Cousin Hew!

'She is more than handsome—she is
downright beautiful! Somewhat of a
brunette, only a very pale and colourless
one, with a small straight nose, dark hazel
eyes, and dark brown hair, and her mouth
is the sweetest in expression I ever saw ;
but I think I see you laughing at all this,
you unbelieving villain !

'Even now, as I write in the library, she
makes a delicious picture, with her beautiful slender throat and shapely head, as she
stands in an oriel, whispering to a canary
which flutters its golden wings against the

bars of its cage, and takes from *her* rosy lips a crumb of sugar in its bill.

'She is frank and open-hearted, and somehow seems to sympathise with all my thoughts and fancies, and we have already gone some length in a mixture of confidential jest and earnest, which, though it may only amuse her, is perilous work to me. She is, perhaps, a little proud of her beauty; but what pretty girl is not? She seems a creature that draws brightness from all around her, while dispensing it in return, and to have been made only to be petted, admired, and caressed.

'You will think that I am hit hard. Well, old fellow, I grant to you that I *am*, and already a remoteness seems to have come over my past—our old barrack-room life at Dumbarton and elsewhere.

'To be hourly in the society of such a girl—to have her daily to walk, to ride, to sing with—is sure to have but one end. Her voice, by the way, is a clear and thrilling soprano—her touch upon the keys is full of tenderness; but a distrust of myself besets me sorely, and leaves unspoken the words that—despite the existence of Cousin Hew—hover on my lips.

' Why ? you will ask.

' Because it is difficult for a man that is poor, and has not even high family to re-commend him, to be deemed other than a fortune-hunter, when he aspires to an un-doubted heiress ; but I shall tell you all about this when I rejoin, and Fate has dropped its pall between her and me.

' I have lost at écarté to Hew Mont-gomerie, and have given him my I.O.U. for a hundred and eighty pounds. Please lend me the money, like a dear old fellow, and I shall square it up somehow, ere we go back to head-quarters, as we are sure to do when the spring drills commence, as I loathe to be in this fellow's debt, and the sum is rather a crusher to me.

' I hope all is right with our detach-ment, and that you grant no passes for more than twenty-four hours, and look sharp after our fellows. I must close now, as we are about to have a spin through the country, as far as Kilwinning, to see the company of archers practise, for old Sir Piers has more than once been captain of the popinjay in June, and a winner of the silver arrow.'

He had closed and despatched his letter ere he remembered that he had omitted all mention, even by name, of Annabelle Erroll.

CHAPTER VII.

HEW'S 'MILD PLAY.'

FOTHERINGHAME wrote promptly back to Falconer; his letter contained the 'needful,' and some bantering advice with reference to his love affair.

'For a man in full possession of his senses,' he wrote, 'you are evidently far gone indeed; and if matrimony alone will cure you, and cause thereby the loss of a thorough good fellow to the corps and the service, why the deuce don't you propose, and turn the flank of the cub named Hew, of whose "mild play" I would advise you to beware, especially as écarté is a very

7—2

rooking kind of game. Cut in for the girl, if you are determined to chuck yourself away ; and, if you play your cards in love as well as the cousin does at écarté, she will soon be nestling her blushing cheek on your waistcoat, and scratching her dainty nose on your diamond studs.'

' How can he write thus of such a creature as Mary Montgomerie !' muttered Falconer, indignantly.

' If she has wealth, it is all the better, as you have none,' continued the epistle. ' And as far as name is required, a Falconer is just as good as a Montgomerie, I suppose.'

' I am doubtful if Sir Piers shares this opinion,' thought Falconer ; but, for the future, he resolved to write no more to Fotheringhame on the subject now growing daily nearer his heart.

' When I put on my first red coat,' continued Fotheringhame, ' I resolved, if I married at all, to condescend to nothing less than a young dowager duchess, a peeress in her own right, or an heiress, beautiful as a houri; but none of these have, as yet, come in my way.'

Falconer lost no time in paying Hew, who gave back the I.O.U., and invited him to have his revenge in a little 'mild play' that night in his own room; and the former promised to take it if he could, resolving the while to keep a sharp watch upon his adversary's play.

Falconer had not been without a hint concerning it from Mrs. Garth, who took a motherly interest in him, as a young officer—more than all, as one of her '*own Cameronians*,' as she was wont to call the corps.

'You and Hew sit up very late at night, I fear,' she remarked incidentally; 'smoking, I suppose?'

'Yes.'

'Any play?'

'A little.'

'Take care,' she resumed softly; 'those who play with Hew often lose and seldom win. He is such a—such a very good

player; and young men, I know, are so
foolish at times.'

Had she hinted aught of this to the
general?

Falconer was almost inclined to think
so, as before Fotheringhame's inclosure
came, his somewhat disturbed and pre-
occupied air was noted by his host, who,
drawing him aside, said kindly:

'Look here, Falconer, you seem rather
distrait this morning. I was once a sub
myself, and not always a jolly one; are
you in want of ammunition? If so, say
the word and my purse is at your service
to any amount; and as for repayment,
take your time; "it may be for years, and
it may be for ever," so far as I care,
when obliging a brother officer of my own
corps.'

Thanking the kind old man from his
heart, ·Falconer waived the subject; and
ere the small hours of the night came, he
found himself in Hew Montgomerie's room
seated at a table on which were several
packs of new cards.

The guest of Sir Piers, and the secret admirer of Mary, poor Falconer felt himself constrained to be victimised nightly in his desire to 'stand well,' as the phrase is, even with Hew : thus he veiled his growing suspicions and dislike of the latter, who, when quite sober, for his own purpose, and to win as much as he could from the luckless sub—a fact and system that would have roused the wrath of Sir Piers —also veiled, so far as he could, *his* dislike and jealousy of Cecil ; and thus held over, *pro tem.*, his intended vengeance, if his path or purpose were crossed, though he never forgot the wicked oath by which he had bound himself.

To lose again, as he had lost before, Falconer knew might prove his ruin now ; but he resolved to be wary, and to watch well, and though Hew was a player accustomed to deep and sharp play for years, in whiling away the lonely hours in an Indian bungalow far up-country, he was destined to have his *modus operandi* thoroughly laid bare on this occasion.

Personally, Hew was disposed to be offensive to Falconer; but dissembled, as he was anxious to 'rook' him a little further, and also to mislead him with reference to his own views concerning Sir Piers' ward. Cunning hints did much to achieve this with Cecil, and to curb and perplex the latter, who never forgot the scene in the avenue on the day of his arrival.

Hew began by pressing Falconer to partake of a tall and foaming glass of brandy and soda, of which Tunley had left a supply for them on a side-table, together with a box of havanas.

Hew's room was hung with coloured prints of the hunting field, the paddock, and other horsey subjects, for though no horseman, as we have said, he made up his book upon coming events and betted freely, while his knowledge of whist and écarté was only excelled by that which he possessed of zoology, so far as referred to rats and badgers. But he loved to affect a 'horsey' style; thus his mantelpiece was littered by spurs, whips, riding-gloves, and rusty bits, and pipes, long, short, clay and briar-root ; and in one corner stood a row of boots, the leather tops of which obtained 'their creamy tint,' as he said, 'from being rubbed with champagne and apricot juice—a hint given him by a gentleman-jock of the Royal Hussars.'

'As usual ?' said Hew ; 'écarté, I suppose ?'

'Yes,' replied Falconer, as they lit their cigars ; 'écarté be it.'

'By Jove ! one would require four eyes to play that game.'

Falconer thought that in the present instance eight might be advantageous.

'Five points, and two packs to facilitate the deal,' said Hew, as he quickly shuffled the cards ; Falconer cut them, and the play began.

Falconer affected what he did not feel— but very far from it—an unusually free, easy, and careless manner ; looked at the hunting pictures hung round the room, chatted on indifferent subjects, to lull the suspicions of Hew, and intent on verifying

his own, in which he found a very unexpected assistant in the form of Mary
Montgomerie's pet terrier Snarley, which
had already become reconciled to him—
had taken even a capricious fancy for him
(for which it had been privately kicked
more than once by the amiable Hew); and
now it lay coiled up at his feet, and it was
while stooping from time to time to pat
the dog, that he perceived the latter
come from under the table with a card in
his teeth.

All this while, Hew had been deeply
intent on the points and counters. He
had, however, allowed Falconer, as a lure,
no doubt, to win four games successively,
and as many sovereigns, when he suddenly
proposed to increase the stakes to five
pounds.

'Agreed,' said Falconer, almost to the
other's surprise, he did it so readily; and
the play went briskly on, while he
continued to chat on irrelevant subjects.

'Who was that good-looking young

fellow who took Miss Montgomerie in to dinner this evening?' he asked.

' Good looking? *I* don't think so, but tastes differ. As to who he is, I may say that he comes of a good old county stock —nay, is *the* stock himself—Bickerton of that ilk. You don't set much store on that sort of thing, as I remember,' added Hew, who could never resist saying a disagreeable thing, ' as you didn't seem to care what Falconers you came of, when Sir Piers—a great man for pedigree— spoke about it.'

Cecil Falconer coloured perceptibly at this remark. Hew saw that it *was* a sore subject, and thought to himself:

' Hit him on the raw there, somehow!'

Meanwhile, Falconer looked curiously at him from time to time. Was it the growing regard for Mary Montgomerie that induced him, Cecil Falconer, to dissemble in his bearing towards this fellow, and affect to forget that, but for a chance next to a miracle, by his hands, on that day at the covers, he might now have been a

mutilated, hideous, and blind creature—
blighted in existence and profession for
ever ?

Yes, the influence of Mary alone could
make him act the double part he felt himself to be acting now.

Hew was dealing, and while Falconer
was stooping to pat Snarley, gave himself
—as he had done before—eight cards instead of *five*, some of which he seemed to
drop as if by a blunder, and in mistake
only took up one, leaving the remainder on
the carpet till the hand was played out,
when he skilfully, but not unnoticed, contrived to replace them in the pack.

' When we are married,' said he, with a
nervous chuckle, ' I'll have to drop all this
sort of thing, I suppose.'

' Well, don't *drop* your cards as yet,' replied Falconer, coldly. ' Married—you,
and who ?'

' Mary and I ; it's all arranged, don't
you know ? Oh, by Jove, here is luck !'
he added, looking for a king, and of course
getting one, while the score was growing

heavy against his adversary, and was close on a hundred now.

'Hallo, Mr. Montgomerie!' exclaimed Falconer angrily, as Hew stooped to fish for a dropped card, 'what's the matter?'

'I have dropped a card, by Jove! and that d——d terrier has collared it. Here, Snarley, you brute!'

'You have dropped half-a-dozen, sir!' said Falconer sternly, as he rose from his chair with menace in his eyes.

'I have not!'

'Look for yourself, then.'

'Where?'

'Under the table.'

'By Jove, there *are* cards there!' said Hew, with well simulated surprise, as he hastily picked them up; 'but they were never dropped by me.'

'By who, then?'

To gain time, or avoid reply, Hew addressed himself to his brandy and soda, of which he had imbibed more than enough already.

'Never again shall I play with you'

('you scoundrel,' Cecil was on the point of adding); 'and if I do not expose your play to Sir Piers and the public, it is only because I have a sincere respect for your family. This is my score,' he continued, taking up a memorandum, 'more than one hundred pounds, which I must have paid you, but for this most fortunate discovery, which cancels everything !'

With these words, Falconer tore up the paper and scattered the fragments, while Hew, unsteady in his movements now, clutched the back of his chair with both hands, grew very pale in the face, and literally glared at him with his shifty green eyes.

'You are mistaken, Mr. Falconer,' he said thickly.

'I am *not* mistaken, sir !'

'Come, come ; don't make a d——d row about nothing,' said Hew, coarsely and bluntly ; but as he had no wish, as yet, to push matters to an extremity with Falconer, or drive him to report the occurrence to Sir Piers, he alternately sought to explain, temporise with, and even to bully him, seeking at the same time to retain him in the room for a little space, and un-wired another bottle for his benefit; and Cecil at first thought he was *acting* intoxi-cation as a cover, or excuse, for his recent trickery.

'We mustn't appear to quarrel, you know,' said he, inarticulately, while glaring viciously at Falconer. 'Won't do—bad style of thing—bad form. Keep it dark with Sir Piers,' he added, swaying about as if his heels were on a pivot; 'a bloated old aristocrat—man likely to hop his twig ! Ah! you thought to draw me like a badger about Mary, but won't be drawn by you or any man.'

'Good-night !' cried Cecil, making his escape.

'Goor-right — goor-right !' said Hew, lunging right and left, and nearly knocking over the card-table, while sending after his guest a savage malediction, with an unlit havana in his mouth.

Thus, at first, through the appearance of

Mary's terrier Snarley with a card in his mouth, Falconer had obtained an insight into the cause of his own continued losses, and the steady success of Hew Montgomerie, with whom, of course, he could never play again; and the knowledge of this, together with the disgrace of being unmasked as a gambler and cheat, added to the growing hatred that possessed the other, who did not appear next morning at breakfast, but left a message with Tunley for Sir Piers, to the effect, that he had gone to fulfil an engagement, for a few days' shooting at Bickerton's place, in the adjacent bailiwick of Kyle, and there, doubtless, he would plot mischief for the time to come.

'A jolly good riddance!' thought Falconer, as he recalled with disgust the episode of the last night.

CHAPTER VIII.

'THE LOVE THAT TOOK AN EARLY ROOT.'

EVERAL days had passed now since Cecil Falconer found himself fairly installed as a guest at Eaglescraig.

Hew was still absent, and Falconer thought it strange, if he and Mary were engaged, or lovers in fact, as many a casual remark from Hew had led him to infer, to the great repression of his own secret hopes, that the handsome Russia leather despatch-box, which was stamped with the three *fleurs-de-lis*, and the three annulets of Montgomerie, and which, with the regularity of clockwork, was brought in at breakfast-time by Mr. Tunley, never contained an epistle from him to her.

Cecil naturally supposed that lovers wrote each other daily; but here was a pair who never wrote to each other at all! Cecil gathered a little hope and confidence from the circumstance, till a tormenting doubt suggested that they might have had a lovers' temporary quarrel.

The days passed, we say, and in all that time, while almost hourly enjoying the society of Mary Montgomerie, Falconer had in no way betrayed the growing emotions of his heart; and though markedly attentive, there was nothing approaching loverhood in his conduct or bearing; but it would have been very difficult to convince the absent and vindictive Hew of that fact, as it was a fixed conviction of his, that there was more in everything in this world than met the eye, and that all still waters run deep.

Cecil's face brightened, and his tone softened more, when addressing Mary Montgomerie than they did when he was

with Miss Erroll, or other ladies. There
were no other signs; but her keener perception and more subtle instinct told her
intuitively that he felt a deeper interest in
her than he had yet avowed; and, though
she had many admirers, the consciousness
of this made her heart beat happily, and
gave a little coquetry to her manner, that,
when other men were present, scarcely
pleased Falconer, who thought that
perhaps she was only *amusing* herself
with him in the absence of her ungracious
fiancé.

She was quite a sister of charity, Mary
Montgomerie, in that part of the country,
and sometimes Cecil drove her pony-
carriage on her missions—a tiny basket
carriage, full of gifts for the poor, all of which
were bestowed upon them in a friendly
rather than a charitable way by the
softly-eyed chatelaine of Eaglescraig, who
loved to cultivate thus a link, a bond,
between the cottage and the great house;
and Falconer, no doubt to please her,
never forgot the various relationships and

S—2

names of the recipients of her bounty, and contrived to have always for each man or woman a packet of that peculiar tobacco which they specially affected ; thus he too became a favourite with them all. He never forgot the joy of these little drives, in the deep old lanes of Cunninghame, with such a companion as Mary Montgomerie, nestled together in the tiny ponycarriage, covered by the ample skin of a dreadful man-eater, whom the general's gun had brought down in the swampy Terrai of Nepaul, and the inevitable Snarley coiled up at her pretty feet ; drives in the clear, frosty winter afternoons, when the skies were blue and bright, or flecked by golden cloud, when the distant hills were capped with snow, and the smoke of the steamers in the Firth of Clyde towered straight upward till lost in the pure and ambient air.

Already they felt quite like old friends, these two; they had a thousand topics and views in common, and they became perfectly unconstrained, familiar, and easy

with each other—familiar with a rapidity
that surprised themselves.

Little by little Mary wound her way
quickly round the heart of Cecil Falconer ;
but dread of her relations with Hew
Montgomerie tied up the tongue of the
former more than even the crushing knowledge of his own meagre exchequer did.

She soon discovered that sentiment
which every young officer possesses—a
pride in his regiment, and drew him out
to talk enthusiastically of its achievements
and ancient history, and watched with
pleasure his animated face while he ex-
patiated on a topic so congenial ; though,
to her, in reality, the glories of Her
Majesty's Cameronians had been rendered
long ago a worn-out household theme by
Sir Piers.

When Cecil touched her hand, ever so
gently, she felt every nerve in her body
thrill with that exquisite sensibility which
was a part of her nature. She saw how
his colour changed at times, and *he* saw
how hers did so too ; she felt in her own

heart the hesitation that was in *his* voice,
and, with the quick perception of a young
girl, thought to herself:

'Can it be that—that he loves me—
loves me, and yet dare not say so?' and
then she would think of the sweet love
song of Montrose, about one who 'feared
his fate too much.'

' I know that Cecil Falconer loves me!'
she would whisper to Annabelle Erroll, in
the seclusion of their own particular
sanctum; 'his eyes, his voice, and his
manner all begin to tell me so. Why
does he not speak out? I wish he had
half the fluency and confidence of that oaf
Hew.'

'But Hew knows the wishes, and is
backed by the authority of your kinsman
and guardian, Sir Piers,' replied Annabelle; 'and if any contretemps occurs—you
know——'

'Well—what then?'

' It will only be a thousand pities that
young Falconer ever found his way to
Eaglescraig at all!'

There were more of this opinion than the soft, pretty blonde Annabelle. A curious and subtle change had come over Mary—a change detected only by Mrs. Garth; as for Hew, he had been too obtuse to notice it; and over her fair, soft face, when she was alone, or sunk in reverie, there shone a brighter light than of yore—a happier and yet more thoughtful expression.

Whence was this? thought Mrs. Garth.

'Take care, Mary,' said the old lady one day, when caressingly folding her to her motherly heart, as she was often wont to do; 'my little pet-bird, be wary, for your own sake, and all our sakes.'

'Wary of what?' asked Mary, growing pale as she knew intuitively what was coming.

'Need I tell you—of this young Cameronian.'

'Why, how? fiddlestick! dearest Mrs. Garth; *what* do you fear?'

'Only this, you seem to forget the in-

tentions of your grand-uncle, and the hope
that your cousin Hew—for so we may call
him—has for the future.'

These injunctions and remarks alarmed
and irritated Mary; but they had the
effect of rendering her somewhat shy or
constrained when with Falconer. The
duets at the piano nearly ceased, then a
cold, or a headache, or some such reason
was urged why the drives in the pony-
carriage should also cease, and they were
abruptly relinquished. There was a little
change; Falconer felt it and was a little
piqued; he remembered her wealth, and
the scene in the avenue, and strove to
crush out of his heart the thoughts he had
been cherishing there. His short term of
leave would soon be at an end; but could
he go back to the dull routine of duty
with this new secret of his soul un-
told?

Even if he won her love, his immediate
idea of the future was vague and shadowy.
It seemed to be chiefly the desire to know
that she was his own, and would be so

irrevocably; to have the sole right of
caressing, doating upon, and worshipping
her; but when marriage and fortune came
to be considered, the deep gulf yawned
again between them, and the cold hardness
of practical everyday life jarred terribly
with the soft suggestions of love, tenderness, and romance.

Should he consult Mrs. Garth, who
seemed so kindly disposed towards him, or
should he first seek the consent of Sir
Piers? No; he felt very timid somehow,
and shrunk from the too probable crushing refusal, or biting inquiry as to the
settlements he could make, his family,
and so forth; he thought that he would
rather try his fate with Mary herself, and
'put it to the touch to win or lose it
all!'

He was already 'so far gone,' as
Fotheringhame would have phrased it,
that his happiness or misery was now
simply the question. He made up his
mind, or thought he did so, to declare his
love to Mary, and he passed several hours

in flattering, and anon in torturing himself by putting every imaginable construction on all that had ever passed between him and her, and between her and Hew, and all that the latter had said to him, suggested to him, and artfully led him to infer.

Luncheon—or 'tiffin' as the general always named it—was over, when one day Cecil, his soul fraught with a declaration, rose to follow Mary, who had gone into the library to look after the last parcel of books from Edinburgh; but ere he could join her he was button-holed by the inevitable general, and the opportunity was lost—perhaps luckily so—who knows?

'One glass more of Lafitte ere you leave me, Falconer,' said Sir Piers; 'are you going to take your gun?'

'No; I walked too far after the birds yesterday, and have rather knocked myself up.'

'You are too young a soldier to say this, Falconer. Knocked up—by Jove, sir!' exclaimed Sir Piers. 'Precisely this day twenty years ago I too was knocked up, but it was not by tramping through covers. It happened thus, you see. We were on the march from the banks of the Chumbul in Malwah, and the rain was incessant— yes, as if the windows of heaven were opened again. I was escorting prisoners, with some native infantry, and had to push on without food or natural rest, and exposed the while to incessant attacks from the Bheels, a savage mountain banditti, who practise human sacrifices in secret, and who were artfully incited to mischief by Holkar; and there was the very devil to pay when we came to the Chumbul Nullah, a terrible torrent, swollen by the rains—no rice for the men, no grain for the horses, which left their shoes, when the nails declined to remain, in the mud. Heavy firing on all hands, the infernal Bheels with their matchlocks and jingals, and the elephants, under it all, trying to carry over the troops; when wounded the brutes became furious, shook prisoners and escort, soldiers' wives and soldiers' children,

baggage, treasure, and everything out of
the howdahs into the foaming torrent, and
a horrible scene ensued—all who got ashore
were massacred, save myself, and I only
escaped by a perfect miracle. It happened
this way, you see——' ·

How Sir Piers was saved Falconer never
learned, for just then he contrived to make
his escape, as Mr. John Balderstone, with
a bundle of legal-looking documents, was
announced on important business, and
arrested the attention of the narrator.

Partly worried by the general's prosy
interruption, and thus partly thwarted in
his purpose, Cecil entered the library, unheard by its occupant; its floor was
covered by rare tiger skins, sent home
from India by the general, who had been a
mighty hunter there, and had transmitted
home enough of them to stock a bazaar,
with their claws set in gold, as necklaces,
ear-rings, and brooches to all the ladies of
his acquaintance.

After one brief glance at the stately
room, with its curtained bay windows, its

walls covered by glittering volumes in splendid oak cases, its marble busts, easy chairs, and reading tables littered with papers, periodicals, prints, and drawing materials, Falconer's eye rested upon Mary Montgomerie, and his heart, full of love though it was, sank as he gazed—gazed on her in all her rare beauty.

She stood before the stately fireplace, looking intently into the bright flame, seeing castles in the embers perhaps, and a sense, momentarily akin to despair, stole over him; her graceful figure was so elegantly and richly attired in a costume so perfect in all its details and ornaments, from the tiny pearl comb that held up the close silky coils of her dark-brown hair, to the beautifully embroidered little slipper that rested on the fender—all indicated the gulf, that, though love might span it, too surely lay between them—a gulf formed by great wealth, by family and high position on her side, and by the utter lack of these three important elements on his own.

He had followed her here, fraught with a proposal, and now he could but ask himself, Why had Fate brought him to Eaglescraig?

She turned suddenly, and welcomed him by a smile, a book in one white hand, the other resting on the mantelpiece, and he was half relieved—so unstable was he of purpose—when Annabelle Erroll issued from the recess of a window, saying:

'Oh, Mr. Falconer, you are just come here when I wanted you—so particularly, too.'

'I am glad of that—in what can I serve you?'

'By writing your autograph in my " Birth-day Book," ' she replied, producing one of the records with which young ladies are wont to bore their friends—a handsomely bound little volume—a bijou freak of the time, wherein a motto from a poet, or a text from Scripture, was appended to each day of the twelve months. 'What is your birthday?'

'The fifth of November.'

'Gunpowder-plot day!' she exclaimed, laughing, as her quick little hand selected the page. 'Here it is—November 5—St. Bertille's day; and the motto is, "Man that is born of woman is of few days, and full of trouble."'

'Scriptural—but rather uncomfortable,' said Falconer, smiling, as he assumed a pen.

'Your days have not been days of trouble surely?' said Miss Montgomerie to him softly.

'My past days have not been without it,' replied Falconer, as a shade crossed his handsome face.

'And your future?'

'Heaven alone knows that—it depends upon another—not *myself*,' said he, with a brief soft glance that made her colour deepen and her eyelids droop, while he wrote his autograph immediately under that of Sir Piers, whose natal day was also the 5th—dedicated to the memory of Guy Fawkes and Inkermann.

'Cecil!' said Annabelle; 'such a pretty name it is—was it your father's name too?'

'No—I am named from my mother, in a way; her name was Cecilia.'

'How strange?'

'There is nothing strange in it at all,' rejoined Falconer gravely, and Mary could perceive that he coloured almost painfully, and the subject was instantly changed by her; yet it impressed her so much, that she mentioned the incident to her confidante and constant guide, old Mrs. Garth.

'Named from his mother, and he has never been known to mention his father,' thought Mrs. Garth; 'there is some painful mystery here—and all mysteries are decidedly unpleasant! I must endeavour to arrest the progress of this *affair*, for the sake of both, ere it is too late! But how to do it, with sufficient tact and delicacy?'

And in this intention she had been further armed by the advice and opinion of Mr. John Balderstone, an old and valued friend and adherent of the Eaglescraig family, who had not been unobservant of the matter in question.

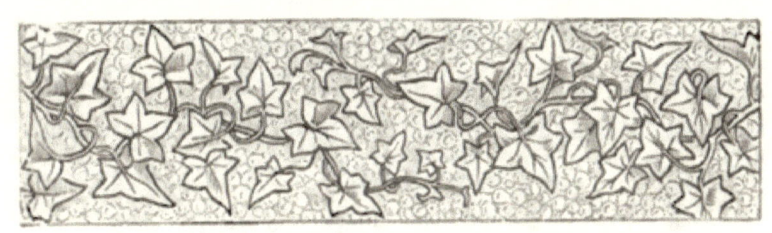

CHAPTER IX.

MRS. GARTH ACTS A FRIENDLY PART.

NOR was the opportunity she wished for long in coming, in the many chances afforded by propinquity, and a residence in the same house; though, in one full of guests, it was difficult to get the object of her solicitude alone.

That afternoon, in the drawing-room, Cecil Falconer and Mary were at the piano; the general preparing for a visit to his stables, as it was rainy, and none could go far abroad; Annabelle Erroll and a few other visitors were idling over books of prints, albums, and other trifles; and

Mrs. Garth, observant of the two first-
named, with something of sadness and
impatience in her heart, was in her usual
seat near the fireplace, sheltered from the
heat by a plate-glass screen, and knitting
busily, for she was always knitting as if
her livelihood depended upon it—but her
industry was all devoted to the comforts of
the poor, for she had a kind heart, having
known much suffering ' in her time,' as she
was wont to say, and thus was ever ready,
so far as her slender means went, to aid
those who were necessitous, or troubled in
any way.

She was tall and thin in figure, and not
without dignity in her bearing, with a look
of calm and patient waiting in her soft
and gentle eyes, which were clear and bright
as those of a young girl, albeit her face
was wrinkled and her silky hair was grey.
Sometimes their expression seemed cold
and sad, when her thoughts travelled back-
ward into the past; yet no eyes could
laugh in expression more merrily than
hers, at times.

Like Sir Piers, and most old people, she lived more in the past than the present, and he, just then, with his feet planted on the hearthrug, while listening with a pleasant smile to an Italian duet, of which he did not understand one word, was busy with that most tantalising of all mental exercises, groping amid vanished years for some fugitive reminiscence that the face and voice of Cecil Falconer had summoned up.

Was it his old comrade Garth he resembled, or who? But Sir Piers had seen and known so many men in his time, that day-dreams of them were no cause for marvel.

'How the time passes!' said he, looking smilingly down on the old lady; 'yet I can remember you a charming girl, when you joined the Cameronians, Mrs. Garth; and that was not yesterday!'

'Well, general,' replied the widow, with a gratified smile on her old face, 'there were worse-looking girls, I dare say, and I had more than one offer before I was

twenty ; but I preferred poor John Garth
to all the world.'

' And right you were—right you were !'
said Sir Piers, emphatically. ' Poor John
Garth ! I shall never forget his fine conduct on the morning we stormed the hill-
fort of the Nabob Ali Nazir-jung (or the
victorious in war), as he boasted himself,
in the Doab between the Jhelum and the
Chenab. It was a strange affair,' he continued, relating an anecdote as well known
to Mrs. Garth as to himself, yet to which
she listened with a kindling eye, ' we sunk
our half-sap by degrees and pushed it close
to the outworks, covering our men by
gabions, sand-bags, and mantelets, and the
assault was to take place an hour before
gunfire, or daybreak. I remember how
lovely the night was ! A breeze stole up
the hillside and stirred the golden bells of
the scented baubul-trees ; the moon in her
silver glory, like a round shield, was
mirrored in the bosom of the Jhelum, and
the stormers were beginning to creep into
the advanced trench, where we could see

their bayonets glittering and their white puggarees behind the shade of the gabions. Just as Jack Garth and I were having a farewell cheroot and drain of brandy-pawnee, Drake, of the Bengal Infantry, who had been detailed to lead the assault, came into our tent looking pale as a sheeted ghost.

'Now Drake was no coward, he had been under fire many times in open ground ; but somehow he felt that to lead a forlorn hope was a very different thing ; in short, almost certain death ; and having led a wild, terrible, irregular, and most irreligious life, his whole soul had suddenly become filled with an uncontrollable dread and dismay of the impending future.

' He told us of the strange emotion that possessed him—he seemed somehow not to care of making a secret of it, to us at least —and Garth instantly and cheerfully offered to take his place, and Drake was to join the covering force. The brigadier commanding permitted the exchange; the place was carried by storm at a wild and headlong rush; Jack Garth, leading the escalade like a hero, reached the heart of the fort untouched, while poor Drake, after the affair was deemed entirely over, and the firing had ceased, was killed by a random shot that came no one knew precisely from where.'

By the time the general had ended his anecdote, and betaken him to the stables to inspect the hock sinews of Mary's favourite pad, of which Pastern, the groom, had made some evil report, the duet was over.

Mrs. Garth had detected the mutual tenderness in tone and expression of eye as it ended, and when the singers left the piano, she resolved to lose no time in seeking to avert, if she could, the trouble which she feared was impending. Not that she loved Hew Montgomerie, but she thought alone of Mary's interests and the wishes of Sir Piers, her oldest, kindest, and best of friends.

But now, when Cecil Falconer ap-

proached her, she thought, as Sir Piers
had done more than once :

'What is there in this young fellow's
face that touches, that interests me ?
Where have I seen that look before ? In
India, I doubt not.'

'I heard the general's anecdote of your
husband, Mrs. Garth, even while we were
singing,' said he, bending over the old
lady's chair; 'he must have been a fine
old officer, and I can assure you that his
memory is still fresh in the regiment.'

Her face brightened with genuine
pleasure as he said this, and her eyes
filled with tears.

'You see the relic I wear of him,' said
the widow, placing her hand affectionately
upon a brooch she wore on her heart, a
silver sphinx, which had whilom been a
regimental ornament, but which she would
not have exchanged for the regal brooch of
Lorne ; 'and now, if you will come with
me, I shall show you his portrait.'

'Thanks,' replied Cecil, and a parting
glance was exchanged between him and

Mary as he left the room and followed
Mrs. Garth across a corridor, hung, like
many other parts of the house, with Indian
trophies of war and the chase.

Falconer thought he was only to hear
about her past and pet memories of the
corps ; but he did not foresee that he must
hear much more that he would rather not
have heard at all. Nor could he suspect
that her primary object was to get him
alone for her own well-meant purpose, or,
as she deemed it, his future peace of mind
and the welfare of Mary Montgomerie.

'This is my peculiar sanctum, Mr.
Falconer,' said she, when ushering him
into a cosily and handsomely-furnished
parlour, 'and here I keep all my relics of
the dead and of other times, and have done
so since I found a happy and contented
home in Eaglescraig,' she added, glancing
at an old iron-bound baggage-trunk that
had been at Bengal, China, Bermuda, and
all round the world with the Cameronians,
and at two regimental swords crossed upon
the wall : one the weapon of her husband,

the other that of her son, a joyous boyish
ensign, who had fallen in a vile skirmish
with a hill-tribe ; shot under the colours,
on a day when match-lock balls were flying
thick, and 'human lives were lavished
everywhere.'

And there now hung the sword that had
failed him in the hot hour of trial.

Over the old but handsome face of Mrs.
Garth, there spread an expression of sweetness and sadness mingled, as she showed
Falconer the miniatures of her husband
and their dead soldier-son ; the latter as an
infant, with a lock of his golden hair,
which she had worn at her heart for twenty
years and more, treasured, like all his
school-boy letters, in the sad but loving
superstition of the heart, in memory of
him and of that day when the troops fell
in and he went with the Cameronians 'to
the front,' to be brought back to her across
six muskets, mortally wounded, to die,
while calling on her name, thanking her
for her love, and dying with his head upon
her breast, as calmly as he had fallen asleep

there when an infant. And so he died thus, as his father had died but a few weeks before him.

'The will of God be done!' said Mrs. Garth, in a sorely broken voice; 'for it was His will that I was to lose them, and that they were to precede me. But Heaven is just, and teaches us that there is a brighter and a better world than this!'

Borne away by her own private or personal sympathies, she almost forgot the purpose for which she had invited Falconer to visit her little sanctum, till he unwillingly recalled it to her memory; as, with all his commiseration for her loneliness, he began to tire of the great many stories she told him of the excellencies of her only daughter—a girl so amiable and so handsome—who had married a curate in the West Indies, a good young fellow, who was so and so, and so and so; of the noble qualities of her son, the poor ensign, and those of the defunct Captain John Garth, who, 'poor dear soul, had been dead and gone—dead and gone—deary me, how—

ever so many years ago.' Thus Cecil—
though there was certainly a cheerful
gossipy quality in Mrs. Garth, that
rendered her a very attractive old lady—
ventured to say :

' And now, Mrs. Garth, you must excuse
me. Miss Montgomerie is expecting me to
attempt that duet over once more with
her, ere we duly perform it for some guests
that come this evening. How sweetly
she sings, and with exquisite taste ! But,
indeed, how perfect she is in all things !'

'A dear child ! I think you admire
her ?' began the widow, now remembering
her task, and suddenly making a leading
remark.

' Admire ! ah, who could fail to admire
her ?' exclaimed Falconer warmly, and
with kindling eye.

' She is a charming girl—ever was a
sweet child—and I am so happy about her
future, Mr. Falconer,' said Mrs. Garth, re-
suming her knitting, without however
raising her eyes to him she addressed.

' Her future ?'

'With Hew—I mean—you understand me, of course ?'

'Hew ?'

'Yes,' she continued softly and gently, reluctantly, too, for she was loth to give him pain, 'Hew Montgomerie. In her circumstances, and with her wealth and its consequent and contingent responsibilities, it has been with us all an anxious matter, that she should choose well and wisely in the world of marriage ; and thus, with Sir Piers' heir of entail, she will be the tenth Lady Montgomerie, without changing her name ! Curious that, is it not ? It cannot fail to be a most fortunate alliance ; but I shall not intrude upon you, whom we have only had the pleasure of knowing so recently, these private family matters.'

Cecil's heart grew cold as a stone, while he listened and heard Hew's remarks thus corroborated, by what, Mrs. Garth felt with regret, must pain him, but deemed it for his future good to hear.

In reply to some half-muttered inquiry (he could not fashion it as a congratulation)

she, by way of explanation and intended
advice, said distinctly much more than
even Hew had done. She told him, in
detail, of Mary's large fortune; and how
entirely Mary and it were—by the tenor
of her father's will—at the behest of Sir
Piers Montgomerie, whose great and sole
object was to consolidate the wealth of the
family in the person of Hew Caddish
Montgomerie, his heir of entail, who,
even with ancient Eaglescraig alone, would
not be rich, and who would be the tenth
baronet in succession from Sir Hew, who
had been made one for his loyalty and
valour in the battles of Montrose, particularly at Tippermuir, in 1644; and thus,
that even a duke might lay, in vain, his
coronet at the feet of Mary Montgomerie!

Pride of birth, and in his own family, of
the old line of Eaglescraig, almost a col-
lateral one with the House of Eglinton,
had been, from youth, a passion with Sir
Piers—a passion that had caused the ruin
of his only son—and so on, with an earnest
tone, a sad, yet gentle smile, she continued,

for his own good as she supposed, to plant (warningly) certain daggers in the heart of her hearer.

'They do not seem much suited to each other, Miss Montgomerie and her intended,' suggested Falconer in a low voice, after a pause.

'Ah, so you think—so you think; but when "Love's young dream" and the honeymoon are over, they will settle down, I have no doubt, into a very happy, loving, and jog-trot couple.'

'It is well that you have told me all this in time,' said Falconer, preserving his calmness of voice and feature by an incredible effort, for if he had mistrusted Hew he could not mistrust Mrs. Garth, who could have no selfish or sinister object in view; 'and I am—most grateful to you.'

'To me—for what?' asked Mrs. Garth, as if she knew not his meaning, though she never looked up, but continued to knit nervously and fast, with tremulous fingers.

'I was, in fact, beginning to admire the general's ward perhaps too much,' he replied, with a sickly attempt at a laugh; 'but now I must think of her only as the intended bride of another.'

'And learn to laugh over the country-house flirtation.'

'Does she love Mr. Hew Montgomerie?'

'I cannot doubt it; though her ways of showing it are certainly shy and peculiar; but then I see, and have seen, more of him and her than you have done, Mr. Falconer.'

'You are sure she will consent to this marriage?' said Cecil, scarcely knowing what he said.

'Yes, most assuredly; if not now, at a later period, for there is no precise reason for haste, unless it be Hew's Indian appointment.'

A silence ensued for a minute or so, during which Cecil heard only the click of the knitting-needles and the beating of his heart.

'Of what are you thinking?' asked Mrs. Garth, looking up with a smile, and then lowering her eyes again, as the pain she read in his face distressed her.

'I am thinking how to collect my ideas,' said he, in a broken voice; 'to reflect on my position, and the information you have given me, with the useful warning contained in it. In two or three days more my leave will be up, and I shall have, inexorably, to depart from a house in which the happiest moments of my life have been spent; yet, which I would to Heaven I had never entered!'

Then, as he left her, Mrs. Garth felt that all her suspicions had been justified; yet, with him, she approached the subject no more.

'I have done the deed! as Macbeth says,' thought she, looking after him; 'poor fellow—poor dear fellow! He seems sorely cut up; but it is all for the best— all for the best! How sad his handsome face looked: and of *whom* does that face remind me? My own dear boy's surely!'

Cecil Falconer was full of jealous anger and deep mortification. He could not, in his present mood of mind, rejoin Mary

Montgomerie, and so he took himself to
the loneliest part of the garden to smoke
and think—to have that universal panacea
to all men in trouble, doubt, or difficulties
—a mild 'weed.' Moreover, there is a
solitude we are prone to seek at times,
even amid our fondest affections.

A tender love for Mary had grown in
his heart; but—apart from a meagre
exchequer—his lack of family rank was
painfully thrust upon him now by every
word Mrs. Garth had, he thought, uncon-
sciously uttered.

In his lonely hours, like most young
men of imagination and of those given to
day-dreaming, he had been wont—though
well-nigh nameless — to identify himself
with the 'Ivanhoes' of romance and
history — the disinherited and disguised
princes of boyish tales, and so forth,
weaving out a brilliant future for himself!
But now!

Now, like Alnaschar in the Arabian
tale, his basket of crystal was smashed;
and yet he could have no future in which

Mary Montgomerie was not to bear an imaginary part.

He was aware that his family pretensions, when judged by the lofty heraldic and genealogical standards of Sir Piers Montgomerie, were as meagre as his monetary could be, and the double consciousness thereof, though failing to influence his heart, had almost utterly fettered his tongue.

These were the reasons why Cecil Falconer did not declare himself as yet, or try conclusions with Hew Montgomerie, but now he had others—more solid and more cruel. It was, however, the old story of the moth and the candle. Mrs. Garth had done much to crush and damp all hope in the heart of Cecil, but could not prevent him from indulging in the perilous charm of Mary's society to the last hours of his now-expiring leave of absence —leave granted 'between returns,' as the technical phrase is.

So that night the duet was not sung, greatly to Mrs. Garth's satisfaction, and somewhat to the surprise and disappointment of Mary Montgomerie, to whom Cecil urged that he was afflicted by a sudden cold, a hoarseness and so forth ; so to his seductive tenor she was unable to make the usually tender soprano replies.

CHAPTER X.

A CRISIS.

EW returned suddenly from Bickerton—Hew of the shifty eyes and cold, fish-like hands— more indignant than ever with 'Old Pipe-clay,' as he irreverently called Sir Piers.

Old Mr. John Balderstone, the family factor, who had been enjoying some shooting at the Bickerton covers, had incidentally and laughingly mentioned having seen Cecil Falconer and Mary Montgomerie twice in her pony-carriage at a considerable distance from home; and thus Hew had returned full of ire at the folly of Sir Piers in having 'invited that fellow

to Eaglescraig,' at the presumption of the
latter, and with his heart full of secret
rage, jealousy, and no little rancour for the
result of the last game at écarté.

Before this time, Cecil perhaps cared
little what Hew said or thought of his
manner with Mary Montgomerie, so far as
friendly intercourse went. Thus Hew had
more than once seen him bending caressingly over Mary as he addressed her,
bending till his dark-brown moustache
almost touched her darker glossy hair.
But then, his whole manner to her might
be described as one long caress, though he
was ever courteous to all women, even the
old and plain-looking; while Mary thought
it new and charming, and something that
even in society she was unused to.

But now there was a sudden change.
The result of Mrs. Garth's friendly advice
was, that doubt, reserve, and smothered
irritation—born of a suspicion that he had
been trifled with, or played with—tinged
the manner of Cecil Falconer, infusing
therein a peculiar strangeness that piqued

Mary Montgomerie, and made their inter-course more perilous, for, being somewhat of a little coquette, it was one of her idiosyncrasies, when so piqued, to avoid a reconciliation that was too openly affected, and shyly, or slyly, to take refuge in those which were merely, and silently, implied.

The communications of the old lady had forced upon him the necessity for sedu-lously seeking to forget, as soon as pos-sible, the existence of Mary; and how far such an effort was consistent with spending the hours of every day in her society, may be imagined.

In the first fever of his spirit he felt in-clined to quit Eaglescraig at once, ere his leave was up, and to get Fotheringhame to telegraph for him; but anon he resolved to linger till the last moment, and sun him-self in the eyes of Mary; and in the midst of all this Hew now returned, like the shadow of evil, to Eaglescraig, suddenly, and not finding either Mary or Cecil in the house, had his spleen further roused on being told by the watchful Mrs. Garth, that they were rambling somewhere in the grounds together.

'In the grounds,' said Hew, viciously; ' where ?'

'I know **not,**' replied Mrs. Garth ; ' but **if you will** absent yourself shooting here and there, Mary must avail herself of the courtesy of others.'

'**Of** course—to help her to water **her** ferns, which she **does** indefatigably, although a staff of gardeners are kept here at Eaglescraig.'

'And to feed her favourite pigeons at the dovecot.'

'How touchingly domestic ; how d——d Arcadian !' said Hew, more viciously than ever. 'Are they on the lawn ?'

'No ; I think they took the path that leads to the grotto,' replied Mrs. Garth, not unwilling to pique the jealousy of **Hew,** who muttered an ugly word, **and at once** left the house to seek them in their ramble.

For this circumstance Sir Piers was in some measure **to** blame, **as** he had desired Mary to show Falconer a curious grotto,

or cavern, **partly** natural and partly arti-
ficial, under the old tower of Eaglescraig,
in which tradition said some centuries ago,
when the wall which had concealed it fell,
a so-called magic lamp had been discovered
hanging from a chain in the rocky roof.
The flame, when first seen, was thought
to be a Jack-o'-lantern, but was found to
proceed from what was supposed to be an
ancient sepulchral lamp, prepared with
matter spontaneously combustible on the
accession of air, and which, instead of burning for centuries, had only taken light
when the grotto was opened.

Be all that as it may, neither Cecil nor
Mary troubled themselves much about the
archæology of the place, though they certainly lingered there, they scarcely knew
why, and she clung to his arm, for the
mouth of the grotto opened inwards from
the rock on which the mansion stood, and
overlooked the Firth of Clyde, three hundred feet below.

Alone with Mary there, Cecil felt that
he was becoming more devoted and

empressé every moment, in spite of his recent resolutions and the warnings of Mrs. Garth.

Their conversation was somewhat disjointed and desultory, especially so far as Cecil was concerned; for the eve of his departure was drawing near; he knew not when, or if ever, he might see Mary Montgomerie again, and the great secret of his heart loaded his tongue. But the faltering accents and broken language of love are generally expressions of the fullest eloquence to her who hears them; and now, filled by all the charm her presence inspired, while gazing into her face which had all the soul-like beauty that radiates from *within*, Cecil Falconer felt his heart flying to his head, and while pressing to his side the little hand that leant upon his arm, he said :

' Another day—only one short day more —and this time of joy, so sweet to me, will have become a thing of the past—a dream—but a past never to be forgotten !'

' I am glad that you have been happy

with **us**—we live so quietly here at Eaglescraig,' she replied, affecting to misunderstand **what he so** evidently referred to.

' Happy indeed ! But who could fail to be happy here ? I am much of a daydreamer, Miss Montgomerie, and often **it** has seemed to me, in my solitary moments and thoughtful moods, that some mysterious sympathy **or** bond was linking my existence **with** that of another, but who that other was I knew not.'

' A strange idea !'

' You will smile at my folly, as **you** no doubt deem it. So, too, have I thought there **was** something singularly sweet in the **idea**, but sweeter still now that .I know, the soul that I dreamed of was *you.'*

Mary's **hand** trembled on his arm, but she **made no reply**, and stood with halfaverted face.

' My lips have been silent,' he resumed, bending **over her, as** she still further averted her face and looked down ; ' yet

you must have guessed the cherished hope
of my heart, and learned, even from my
glance—that I—that—that I love you !'

So Mrs. Garth's friendly warnings all
came to nothing, and even Hew's existence
was forgotten !

' I saw from the first,' said Mary, in a
low and agitated voice, ' from the first, that
you admired me, but—but, I never thought
that——'

' That I loved you ?'

' I know not what I thought.'

' Oh, Mary—may I call you so ?—I
have no words to tell you, Mary, darling,
how fondly, how deeply and tenderly I
love you !'

Her hands were in his now, and her
long lashes were cast down, during a little
pause that ensued, and he could see her
soft bosom heaving under her dress.

Then she looked up with a coy, shy
smile of great brightness, as she asked :

' Am I the first you have loved—the
very first ?'

' Fancies I have had—as what lad has

not—but I never loved till now, Mary,'
he replied, with great tenderness, 'unless
it was the love I bore my poor mother,
who is now in her grave.'

' I am so confused—so startled, Mr.
Falconer.'

' Do say " Cecil," I implore you !'

' Well, then—Cecil.'

· No need to say more just then, as their
lips met, passionately for an instant, and
Cecil felt that she was his own. Then
Mary shrank back a little, and blushing
deeply, said :

' Oh, what would Sir Piers say if he
knew of this ?'

There was something of terror in her
tone—alarm, at least, as Cecil thought.

' When I tell him of my love for
you——' he began.

' Oh, that you must not—must not do
—yet awhile, at least !' she exclaimed
earnestly.

' Why, my darling ?'

' Don't ask me—do not ask me ! Be
content that—that——'

'You love me?'

'Oh, Cecil—yes. But your love for me —when did it first begin?' she asked, looking up with the same fond yet shy smile again on her soft face.

'Heaven only knows—when I first saw you, without a doubt,' replied Falconer, drawing her towards him. 'But now tell me, darling——'

Ere he could say more, she shrank from him. A step was heard on the gravelled path, Snarley growled and showed his teeth, and Hew appeared close by them, at the mouth of the grotto—Hew, with a very dubious and mingled expression on his face.

'Have you not heard the gong sound for luncheon?' he asked, curtly and sulkily.

'Hew—returned already!' said Mary, blushing deeply.

'So soon—yes,' said he.

'Had good shooting at Bickerton?' asked Cecil Falconer, feeling that it required a double effort to be complaisant to Hew just then, and to slide into the commonplaces required by society.

'Pretty fairish—knocked over a few rocketters or so. There were ten guns out. But how do *you two* come to be here ?' he asked bluntly and almost rudely.

'Sir Piers requested Miss Montgomerie to show me where an ancient lamp had been found,' replied Cecil, with some annoyance of manner.

Hew muttered something unpleasant under his moustache, as he thought that the 'ancient lamp' had thrown more light on their proceedings than he anticipated, and drawing Mary's arm through his own, he said sharply and curtly :

'Let us go back to the house, or we shall be late.'

Cecil's handsome mouth was compressed with sternness at the abruptness of Hew's bearing, tone, and words. His small and well-cut nostrils quivered, and his eyes flashed with the anger which, despite his recent joy, he felt a difficulty in restraining.

Hew was sharp enough to see this; but feeling himself somewhat master of the situation, and a species of marplot, he gave one of his strange smiles, and said something that might mean anything or nothing, as he appropriated Mary and marched off with her towards the house.

How long he might have been eaves-dropping, and how much or how little of their conversation he might have over-heard, or what he might have overseen, it was impossible for them to conjecture; but extreme annoyance clouded the fair face of Mary, and bitter chagrin was but ill concealed in that of Falconer.

'Pray do not quarrel with Hew,' Mary found opportunity to say in a rapid whis-per; 'you know not his power in the art of scheming, manœuvring, and mischief.'

Cecil felt his heart beat lightly again at the interest in him implied by her words, and the secret understanding they sug-gested and created.

Though we doubt very much if Mr. Hew Caddish Montgomerie ever heard of the Bard of Twickenhem, yet we are certain that he believed with him, that 'every woman is at heart a rake;' and thus he was the more irate with Mary, as he was prone to take the worst view of every one and everything.

As they pursued the circuitous path that led from the grotto to the house, Hew maintained a somewhat sulky silence, as he had neither the good feeling nor the good taste to conceal his annoyance. He, perhaps, loved Mary; but if so, it was after a selfish fashion of his own, and as much as it was in him to love anyone. He knew her fortune to a shilling; he had a passionate, an inherited, and avaricious love of wealth, and he knew right well the vast importance that attached to the possession of it; thus he took Mary to task, the moment Falconer left them—with a glance, which Mary read, though to Hew it was all unseen, or misunderstood.

'Were you and that fellow long in the grounds to-day?' he asked bluntly, and with anger in his eyes.

'What if we were?' was the defiant reply.

'I asked you a question, cousin.'

'One you have no right to ask.'

'No right?'

'None!' said she, with decision.

'Come, I like that! I am your cousin.'

'Nothing more, thank goodness!—and scarcely even that, save by name; and you are not my mentor.'

'If I were so ——'

'Well, sir; if you were?'

'I should say that I was extremely sorry to meet you and Falconer together, as I met you just now.. I consider it most unseemly!'

'Are you my guardian, Hew?' asked the little beauty, with growing irritation.

'Would that I were so, legally!'

'I cannot agree with you,' responded Mary, with a merry laugh.

'I regret to see how this intimacy has grown between you and an utter stranger.'

'Pray what can it matter to you who my gentlemen friends are?'

'How can you adopt this tone to me,

knowing what you do of Sir Piers' intentions, Mary? As for this fellow——'

'Fellow? What has he done to offend you, Hew Montgomerie, that you speak of him in this style?'

'I was only about to remark that, like Oliver Twist, I have no doubt that he can trace his genealogy all the way back to his parents—to his mother, at least, for I suppose he has, or had, such a relative,' was the coarse and bitter sneer of Hew; 'but that measure of ancestry will scarcely suit the standard of Sir Piers Montgomerie.'

Mary remembered the little episode of the 'Birthday Book,' and her heart for a moment sank, and her countenance fell.

'What *do* you mean?' she asked.

'I know—what I know—that is all,' replied Hew, malevolently.

'And I know that you are extremely rude and ill-bred,' said Mary, as she swept away from him, and with difficulty restrained her tears, while Hew looked after her with a scowl that was strangely mingled with a triumphant smile.

He did not knit his eyebrows, for he had little or nothing in that way to knit; but his closely-set eyes twinkled viciously and furtively, as he began to feel that the power he once possessed, or hoped to possess, over Mary, and more especially over her fortune, was slipping away; and the emotions of wounded pride, disappointment, avarice, and an odious passion for her that was not love, grew keenly and stingingly in his heart.

Next day Cecil's leave would be up, and in the interval, so sedulously did Hew keep guard, that never again had Cecil a chance of addressing Mary alone; but the rival, while thus employed, could see with growing rancour that they looked suspiciously amiable and happy, and could talk confidentially enough with their eyes, if prevented from doing so with their tongues; and now, to preclude any fresh invitations on the general's part, or any further extension of the hospitality of Eaglescraig, Hew resolved, ere their guest departed, to do him all the mischief he could with his host.

CHAPTER XI.

HEW MAKES MISCHIEF.

FINDING, as we have shown, that any appeal to Mary Montgomerie was vain, Hew determined, as he muttered, to give the general 'an eye-opener on the subject.'

He knew that 'a jilted suitor is hopelessly and irreparably ridiculous, and that the jilt is apt to score the honours.' Without an engagement existing between them, there could be no jilting in the case of him and Mary, but in his blind, unmeaning hate of Falconer, his jealousy and avarice, he never thought of that; and only considered that the wishes of

Sir Piers and himself, and the object for which he had been deliberately brought home from India, were on the point of being baffled, or set utterly aside, by the intervention of an unexpected interloper, to blacken and defeat whom was but just and right, he deemed on his own part, and in his own behalf.

Without a just cause he had been from the first instinctively the foe of Cecil Falconer; and ill-founded enmities, it is said, are ever the most obstinate and bitter.

He found Sir Piers in the library, lounging in an easy-chair, smoking a beautiful hookah which he had brought with him from India, and deep in the pages of the *Field*.

'Can I have your attention for a little time, Sir Piers?' he asked.

'Yes, my boy; fire away. About what do you wish to speak?'

'A subject very near my heart, as you know,' replied Hew, leaning on the back of the old baronet's chair: 'Mary Montgomerie.'

'God bless the dear girl!' exclaimed Sir Piers, as his brightening eyes were raised inquiringly to Hew's face. 'It is time some arrangement were made by you and her; for Mary deserves the purest and best love the heart of man can offer her.'

'Such love is mine, dear Sir Piers,' whined Hew.

'I hope so.'

'But I come not to speak of that.'

'Of what, then?'

'Of Mary and your new friend, Falconer.'

'Falconer!' exclaimed Sir Piers, staring blankly at Hew through his gold eye-glasses.

'Seriously, sir, it seems to me that, thanks to the propinquity your unwise hospitality has afforded them, Mary is drifting, with that fellow Falconer, the way that many other young ladies have drifted before her.'

'What does this mean?' exclaimed Sir Piers, wheeling his chair sharply round.

' Worry, of course ; and, d—n it ! I am
getting too old to have any worry—had
enough of it in my time, up country ! Has
propinquity not helped you ? Gad, sir, in
my day, I should like to have seen the
biped that could turn my flank with any
girl ; but why the devil don't you push the
trenches yourself ?'

' But don't you think they have become
too intimate ?' asked Hew, with growing
irritation.

' Why ? How ?'

' With all this singing, music, and
philandering.'

' Pooh ! not at all. Let them amuse
themselves. I was once their age. It is
no use making a fuss ; but why the deuce
don't you cut in, and sing, play, and phi-
lander too, as you call it ? Besides, Falconer in a few hours now returns to
Dumbarton, or to headquarters, and there
is an end of it all ! To me, Hew, it seems
natural enough that young Falconer should
be attracted by our Mary ; but aware of
her position, of my views and your wishes,

and more than all, your prospects and rank when I am gone,' he added, glancing at a portrait of his dead son, ' I should very much doubt if she encouraged any particular attention on his part.'

' There I don't agree with you; and when once a girl's heart becomes warped, or interested in a fellow, she cares little what his rank or position may be; and of this Falconer's family or antecedents we know nothing.'

' True, by Jove !' said Sir Piers, whose pet weakness was now interested. ' He seemed not to know, himself, which I thought odd. I wonder what arms he uses ? The Halkertoun family carried *azure*, a falcon *argent* crowned with a ducal crown.'

' Arms !' said Hew, with a mocking laugh. ' If all I suspect be true, his have been quartered and attested by the Blue Bottle Herald and Pimlico Pursuivant. But apart from his dangling after Mary, I have my own reasons for feeling glad that Eaglescraig will soon be rid of him.'

'He is a presentable young fellow—a Cameronian too, and bears her Majesty's commission,' urged Sir Piers in favour of Falconer, whom he really liked; 'but what are the personal reasons you refer to?'

'Because in a little time he would have rooked—ruined me!'

'How?'

'At écarté.'

'At écarté?'

'Yes. Before I went to Bickerton—to keep out of his way, in fact—he inveigled me to play, night after night, when all others had retired. My play is always mild—but his was *wild!* His constant phrase was that it was so *ennuyant* to play for low stakes, so we always doubled, and even trebled, them—I always losing.'

'Why?'

'Because,' replied Hew, deliberately, while a malevolent gleam shot from his parti-coloured eyes, 'it is seldom safe to play écarté, or piquet either, after dinner, and when drinking brandy-and-soda with a fellow who takes nothing—is too wary to do so.'

'And so you have lost?' said Sir Piers, flushing with indignation.

'Fearfully; and I suspect the scoundrel was in the habit of dropping his cards.'

'What!' roared Sir Piers, aghast. 'The devil! Do you say so?' He pinched his gold eyeglasses tighter on his high aristocratic nose, and absolutely glared through them at Hew, as he turned his keen face full round to await what he had to say, and with a face expressive of intense chagrin, disappointment, and dismay.

'I do not say so—I only suspect,' said Hew, afraid that he, in the extremity of his malice, had roused a storm it might be difficult to quell, or see the end of.

'And he is one of the Cameronians!' exclaimed Sir Piers, in an agitated voice. 'Gad! in my time, he would have had his hands tied behind his back, and been drummed to the barrack-gate. Do you actually tell me this? Gambling, in camp or quarters, *I* never permitted for a moment

—they are strictly forbidden by the thirty-fourth paragraph of the sixth section of the Queen's Regulations. But the idea of gambling and cheating at Eaglescraig! D—me, I'll explode! I remember that, when we were cantoned at Jubbulpore, before we were relieved by the Seventy-Eighth, with bag, baggage, and twelve bagpipes——'

'But our play is ended now, Sir Piers— once and for ever!' interrupted Hew, as he shivered at the idea of an Indian anecdote, which was certain to follow whenever Sir Piers mounted his Oriental hobby-horse.

·'Ended; I should think so! But, as we used to say in India, beware of a black Brahmin and a white pariah!'

The point of this aphorism was not very apparent; but Hew, satisfied that he had now completely ruined Cecil Falconer so far as Sir Piers was concerned, was so well pleased that he listened to a sudden Bengal narrative of a thirty days' march, amid the horrors of Dacoits and Thugs, swamps and jungles, tigers and snakes, dismounted guns and broken bones, dead bullocks and swollen rivers; and then, after a pause, during which the baronet had been reflecting with knitted brows, he said:

'But to return to the first subject, Hew. Do you mean to tell me, and do you seriously think, that this—a—a—person, *has* made any undue impression upon her —upon Mary?'

'From my soul I do, sir, and know it to my bitter cost!'

Another angry malediction escaped the general.

'I cannot desire him to leave my house, though right well disposed to do so,' said he; 'but a little time will see him gone now, thank Heaven! I am deeply concerned by what you tell me, my dear Hew; all the more so, that I have been the unwitting means of bringing all this unforeseen mischief to pass.'

'Only an hour ago I interrupted a little scene in the grotto there could be no mistaking! He was bending tenderly over her, and uttering sighs that would have softened the heart of a pawnbroker.'

'Don't use such odious similes, Hew!' exclaimed Sir Piers. 'Whatever may be the personal merits or demerits of this young man,' he continued, with an angry laugh, 'apart from my firm intentions, your wishes, and Mary's own future welfare, it would never do for her to make a *mésalliance*—to throw herself away upon an ambitious adventurer, on whose name there too evidently rests the stain of obscurity, at least. It is well that he is going, Hew! I want no other catastrophe, no second fiasco, to occur to a Montgomerie of Eaglescraig!' he added, with deep and sorrowful frown, as he referred to a family episode we shall have to relate ere long. 'But here comes Mary, most opportunely. Leave us, Hew, and I shall talk with her alone.'

As Hew retired, with disappointed passion and gratified revenge curiously mingled in his face, the thought flashed upon the mind of Sir Piers that expostulation or advice might only prove futile, and, by exciting opposition, make the matter worse (as he had bitterly experienced once before in his life), though he knew not how far the matter had gone, or how deeply love had taken root in the hearts of both Mary and Falconer. Moreover, he thought that as separation, which he deemed a safe cure, was so close at hand, it might be better to ignore the communications of Hew, and let matters, after Falconer's departure, fall into their old routine, yet having the intended marriage of Mary and his heir pressed forward, in spite of all opposition; but now, the sudden and apparently opportune entrance of the fair culprit herself overset his calmer calculations.

CHAPTER XII.

CECIL'S DEPARTURE.

THOUGH indignant at Falconer, Sir Piers could scarcely find it in his heart to be angry with Mary, she was so sweet and winning—his dead kinsman's one ewe lamb, committed to his care. She had been to him as the child of his old age, taking the place of that only son whose death he had never ceased to lament; she, who by her affection, in the thousand nameless little recurring trifles of life, as a tender and loving daughter rather than a grand-niece, had made herself so useful and necessary to him.

Mary had come in search of a book, a passage in which she meant to show Cecil, whom she had left with Annabelle Erroll, when Sir Piers summoned her to his side; and though she saw a gloom on his fine old face, the cause of which she dreaded and suspected to have been Hew, who had just quitted the room, she seated herself on a velvet tabouret, near her guardian's own chair, and nestling at his knee as she had been wont to do when a little girl, she drew one of his shrivelled hands caressingly over her handsome head, and, looking up smilingly, said:

'Well, grand-uncle darling, what have you to say to me?'

'Much, Mary—yet a few words may suffice,' he replied, as the lines faded out of his face. He had at first resolved to be very stern and irate with her; but he reserved all his bitterness for Falconer. 'Am I right when I say that I have been given to understand that Mr. Falconer has forgotten his place as a guest in my house, and dared to address you surreptitiously in language other **than a** mere friend **or** guest may do ?'

At this question, so sententiously put, Mary blushed painfully, and then grew very pale indeed, for her heart was **yet** vibrating with its new-found joy, and the memory of **that kiss**, the **first that** was ever given **her** by any man save old Sir Piers himself.

'Has he attempted to win for himself that **affection which** should belong to another ?'

'Oh, grand-uncle, what do you mean ?' asked Mary piteously, **and** feeling quite overwhelmed.

'What I ask, Mary; and I **wish** you **to** know, further, that he is everyway unworthy the consideration of any girl— wholly unworthy the kindness I have wasted on him.'

'Unworthy !' repeated Mary, faintly; and yet her heart rebelled, for she now recognised the malevolent influence of Hew.

'I have other **views** for your future, as

you know, dear Mary — views long cherished and most dear to me, and I am not going to have my plans and prospects marred by a fortune-hunting subaltern and a romantic girl's folly. Understand me, Mary, and the power your father's will has given me over you and your fortune.'

Mary remained silent, but tears welled up in her eyes—tears that sprang from emotions of anger as much as annoyance and intense mortification.

'I don't object to the fellow because he is a subaltern, with little, if anything, more than his pay,' said Sir Piers, as if ashamed of using the military rank as an adjective; 'but I do object to this, Mary, as your guardian and only kinsman, in whose hands the whole of your fortune is vested, to bestow, so far as possible, on my heir of entail, who is to share it with you. But here, if all I am told is true, you have been tempted—you, with beauty and attractions that might win a coronet—you, with an inheritance, and certainly with a name, second to none in Scotland—to cast

your lot, perhaps, with one destitute of
position, save that which a commission
gives him—one without family or friends
either, so far as we know,' continued the
general, musing, or talking himself into a
fit of anger ; 'as Hew has hinted, the first
of his race—a gambler, too——'

'A gambler, grand-uncle ?'

'A gambler—and worse—who has sorely
fleeced poor Hew ! But I shall amply re-
imburse him, as it was by my old-fashioned
folly our unlucky guest came here. How
I shall be able to receive him at dinner to-
day I scarcely know, for now I consider
his presence in Eaglescraig an insult. You
may have been foolish—girlish, Mary ; but
I know that you won't further vex your old
grand-uncle, who loves you so, but will
sedulously avoid or shun this person, Falconer, during the few hours he is under
our roof : and when he leaves it let his
existence be to you as a thing of the past
—as that of the dead—but the dead who
are forgotten !'

And with this cruel advice, which was all

the more cruel and impressive from being coolly, calmly, and deliberately given, the general rose and quitted the library, leaving Mary in a flood of tears and quite over-whelmed with dismay ; not at the invec-tives bestowed upon Falconer, as she knew their source and true value, but at the hostility so suddenly developed by Sir Piers, and the long term of domestic misery she saw before her in the future.

But, as indignation swelled in her heart against Hew, she dried her tears and gathered a courage from her growing anger. Yet she drew her breath with difficulty, and pressed a hand upon her side as if a pang of pain was there.

Unaware of all this scene, Falconer, even in the face of his approaching departure, was chatting away gaily with Annabelle Erroll, and having the full assurance of Mary's love, seemed to tread on air, and feel emotions only of gratitude and joy. He was as sure that Mary was not a girl to love lightly as he was sure that she had given her whole heart to him, despite the fiat, the 'general order' of Sir Piers, that was to assign her as a bride to Hew Montgomerie.

When the little circle assembled for dinner, the last of which he was to partake in Eaglescraig, Cecil became suddenly and painfully sensible that some change had come over all present, save Miss Erroll.

Though all were scrupulously polite, their old cordiality seemed to have evaporated!

Hew was colder than ever; not that Cecil Falconer cared much for that, but he felt that the usually chatty and genial Sir Piers was cold in manner too, and haughty and monosyllabic, for a time; and Cecil recalled the cordial welcome of his first night in that hospitable mansion, when his old host insisted on escorting him to 'his quarters,' as he called his room, singing his old Indian song about 'half-batta' as they went. He felt the change keenly, and angrily too, all the more that he failed to understand it.

'What the deuce does the general suspect—what does he know?' thought Cecil, whose own suspicions certainly pointed towards Hew; but he and Mary were without the means of comparing notes together, or even of taking of each other the tender farewell they would have wished.

At table—with the memory of all that had passed in the library—she was nervous, silent and reserved, while she kept listening to the voice and looking furtively in the eyes that as secretly sought hers—the voice and eyes she had been bidden to forget as those of ' the forgotten dead.'

When the ladies withdrew, the general, who was the soul of hospitality, when pushing the decanters round—for he was vain of his clarets, Chateau Lafitte, Haut Brion, and Margaux—felt half inclined to relax and relent at times. Could Hew have been mistaken in that diabolical story about the cards? But if so, he was not mistaken on the subject of Falconer's admiration of his intended wife; and though such was utterly adverse to the wish of Sir Piers, he felt that he could forgive it,

especially as, like Mrs. Garth, he felt that
in the look and air, the expression of face,
and bearing of Cecil Falconer, there were
an undefinable something that brought
painfully back to memory the face of
another; and yet, between the two faces,
that of his dead son—for his it was—and
the face of Falconer, there was no especial
likeness.

'Had poor Piers been living now,
thought the general, 'he would have been
nearly fifty years of age, which reminds me
that I am getting too old to harbour
thoughts of anger now.'

In the drawing-room, Cecil found the
piano closed; there was evidently to be no
music that evening, nor was he in the mood
for it, except in so far that it might have
served to cloak a few farewell words to
Mary, whom he found occupied at chess
with Mrs. Garth, and save that she trembled a little and changed colour at his
entrance, she seemed unconscious of his
presence, as the slow and silent game proceeded in its tedium: and leaving Sir

Piers and Hew deep in some matter of local improvements to be made on a certain farm, he seated himself beside Miss Erroll, on an ottoman, a little way apart.

'And so you indeed go to-morrow?' she observed, for lack of something else to say apparently.

'Inexorably, Miss Erroll,' he replied, with a smile that was no smile at all; 'and after all the happiness I have enjoyed here I shall feel doubly lonely at Dumbarton, as it is most probable that the general may invite my brother officer here, to take my place.'

'Mr. Leslie Fotheringhame?' she said in a low voice, while her eyes drooped.

'Yes.'

'What leads you to think so?' she asked, with a little agitation of manner that Cecil could not fail to detect.

'He has once or twice said such was his intention.'

Such, indeed, had been the general's wish, but recent events had made him change his mind.

Miss Erroll was a singularly attractive and bright-looking girl—bright in her manner and blonde beauty. Her fair, golden hair rippled back from her broad, low, snowy forehead ; and she had a tender, rosebud-like mouth, and very lovely eyes. In the full preoccupation of his thoughts with Mary, Cecil Falconer had not been quite conscious that on several occasions Miss Erroll had led him to talk of his solitary friend at Dumbarton, Leslie Fothering-hame, as if she had some interest in him ; and also, that if he attempted to question her on the subject, she skilfully or nervously changed it, or evaded it.

'You know Fotheringhame, it would seem ?' he asked.

'I do—or *did*, rather,' she replied, in a low voice.

This implied that there had been a coolness, a quarrel, or a dropping of acquaintance somehow.

'He was not always in the Cameronians,' said Falconer.

'I am aware of that.'

' Perhaps you knew him when in his former regiment ?'

' When in his former regiment—yes,' she replied, repeating his words, as if afraid to trust herself to any of her own. ' How long will Mary puzzle over her king ?—she is quite checkmated !' she said with a forced laugh, as she moved towards the chess-table, to conceal from Falconer an expression of genuine pain that shot over her soft, fair face.

He noticed now an unmistakable agitation of manner and sudden sadness of eye and tone in Annabelle Erroll; and though he almost immediately forgot this amid the anxiety of his own love affair, he remembered it all at a future time.

The brief evening that followed the late and fashionable dinner-hour passed rapidly —too rapidly for Cecil ; yet heavily withal. The evening was so unlike its predecessors, for the once pleasant circle seemed entirely changed. How Falconer's heart would have swollen with just rage had he known the reason why !

And this was his last night at Eagles-craig; it seemed as if he was looking on everything there for the last time, Mary's pale face included, and the time came at last when he had to say to her:

'Good-night, and good-bye, Miss Montgomerie.'

Yet Fate was not so cruel as to make them part thus, for through a skilful manœuvre executed by Miss Erroll—in compelling Hew to hold a folio book of Indian photographs while the general explained to her something therein—as Mary gave Cecil her hand, 'her soft, white virgin hand, that had never touched aught to soil or harden it,' he whispered hurriedly, and unheard by all save her:

'Good-bye. Oh, my darling, my own Mary! How am I to live without you, how make the time pass till we meet again —if ever?'

And eye conveyed to eye and heart, a world that was alike unsaid and unseen.

Courtesy compelled him to shake the

damp, limp hand of Hew, and the shifty eyes of the latter looked radiant with malevolence and triumph.

Grey dawn was breaking, and save Mr. Tunley, the butler, and a sleepy valet, all the household were sunk in slumber, when Falconer, after an almost sleepless night, and feeling as if it must be some other person and not himself that was about to depart, got into the dog-cart with his portmanteaus and gun-case.

A cold, chilly morning, the last day of January. The crocus formed a golden band along the parterres of the terrace; a few snow-flakes came aslant the dull grey sky, and the robin redbreast, his little heart filled at least with hope, twittered and sung on the bare spray, where the first buds of spring would soon be bursting. All around the landscape looked dank and barren and dreary—unusually so it seemed to Cecil's eye.

Pate Pastern, a groom, drove the dog-cart. Hew had again flatly declined to do

so, saying overnight to Sir Piers that he
'didn't care to drive a fellow like Falconer,
a fellow so devilish sharp at cards, and all
that sort of thing, you know;' and the
general had said approvingly :

'Of course not, of course not, my dear
boy.'

Cecil's mind was a prey to great bitterness in the conviction that he was leaving
Eaglescraig, as it seemed, for ever, and
with no definite plans, views, or hopes for
the future. Was all this new love, this
new joy, to pass out of his life and out of
hers as suddenly as it had come to
them ?

It seemed so !

He had, he thought, done wrong in
winning the heart of Mary Montgomerie
without the permission of her proud old
guardian and kinsman ; but now he had
little compunction for having done so, as
that permission would never have been
accorded to him, and he felt that his departure seemed a welcome move to all but her
—a departure permitted to pass coldly, and

without even a well-bred expression of regret.

A farewell glance at the stately modern villa, and the grim old keep that towered behind it, showed him their walls all reddened in the early morning sun; the window-blinds close drawn, all closed as yet, save one. His heart told him it was that of Mary's room. The sash remained, of course, unlifted, but the blue silk curtain was festooned back, and every pulse vibrated within him when he saw the wave of a white handkerchief, just as the dog-cart went bowling down the wooded avenue towards the highway.

It was Mary's farewell to him.

Would the strains of the sweet old story, that never tires, come to their ears again? How would it all end between him and Mary Montgomerie, or was it ended *now*?

CHAPTER XIII.

IN SHADOW LAND.

' I AM truly glad for Hew's sake, and for Mary's sake, that he has gone—gone ere it was too late !' thought Sir Piers, as he sat in his easy-chair in the library that afternoon, when nothing remained of Cecil Falconer at Eaglescraig but an aching pain in Mary's heart, and in the avenue the ruts of the wheels that had borne him away.

His recent conversation with Hew about the dread of a *mésalliance* made the old baronet's mind revert—as it too often did, bitterly and unavailingly—to another *mésalliance* in his family, which nearly brought ruin—for such in the vanity of his soul he deemed disgrace—upon the Montgomeries of Eaglescraig, who had for ages been a power in the bailiwick of Cunninghame.

' It seems a pity that we should disturb the stagnant waters of that Dead Lake which men call the Past,' says Miss Braddon; but Sir Piers was rather prone to do so ; and now, as he sat gazing into the red, clear, burning embers, they seemed to take divers shapes and forms, quaint and curious pictures, of which, in reality, he saw little, for his thoughts were treading upon each other fast, and in his dreamy yet steadfast gaze there was a fixed, a far-off look—a look in Shadowland.

A childless old man, he was thinking of what was now, and all that might have been, but for his own stubborn will and pride of heart.

Some five-and-twenty years before this time, he had a son who had been the pride of that heart, and valued all the more as being the only child of a young and beautiful wife, after whose death he had never married again, but sought relief from thought amid the wars of British India.

From his infancy young Piers had been petted in every way, and was in some respects the spoiled child of the household. He grew up a bright and handsome lad, full of intelligence and enthusiasm for music and painting; but to dabble in these, even as an amateur, Sir Piers deemed unworthy of his family, so in due time he had his son gazetted to the Cameronians, then in garrison at Gibraltar.

During the unhealthy season, which lasts there from July to November, when the east winds come surcharged with moisture, young Piers was seized with fever, and obtaining leave of absence, went to travel in Italy, and his letters that came from thence to Eaglescraig, detailing his adventures and journeys up Calabrian mountains and through defiles in the Abruzzi, all indicative of returning health and strength, filled the heart of his father with joy, as his son, the heir of his house and name, was the veritable apple of his eye.

His letters from Rome teemed with his enthusiasm about the objects of history, the ruins of the past, and his ecstasies over the treasures of the innumerable *studii* of painting and sculpture ; and then came much about a painter whose acquaintance he had made at the Academy of San Luca, and whose daughter was one of the most beautiful girls and accomplished musicians in that city of pilgrimage to all lovers of art.

After this Sir Piers grew painfully and suspiciously conscious of the fact that his son's correspondence became irregular, his epistles constrained and brief, while more than one incidental reference to the artist's handsome daughter caused alarm in the parental heart, all the more as young Piers had said that her father, 'though a man of humble origin, was an emperor among artists.'

'Piers,' said the baronet to his confidential friend and local factotum, John

Balderstone, 'refers to this girl oftener than I quite relish or like ; and his letters are vague and odd as—if—as if—he had something to conceal. I wish he were back to his regiment at Gibraltar.'

'Young men *will* be young men,' replied the other ; 'the girl may have picked up some pretty tricks of foreign manners, and thus interested him.'

'There are four months of his leave to run ; surely he will not spend them all among these painter-fellows in Rome ?' said the baronet, grimly.

For one moment, however, an idea of what was really the case never entered the haughty mind of Sir Piers Montgomerie. He only feared an entanglement — as a subaltern, he had often been in such scrapes himself—but nothing *more !*

And now a month elapsed without any letter from Rome, and genuine anxiety filled the mind of Sir Piers, whom a temporary illness confined at Eaglescraig, and prevented from coming swoop down upon his son in the Eternal City, and seeing how 'matters were' for himself.

At that very time there arrived at a country hotel, within a few miles of Eaglescraig, a young married pair, with a valet and a little French soubrette. Both were singularly handsome—the lady, indeed, was a very beautiful girl with minute and delicate features, dark eyes and rich brown hair; and in her husband, whose face and figure were alike striking, but for the ample beard he now wore, the people of the hotel would have had little trouble in recognising young Piers Montgomerie, for he it was, with his bride, the penniless daughter of 'the emperor among artists!'

He was one who could scarcely fail to make himself agreeable to all women, as he excelled in that half-flirting manner which some young men can cultivate with skill; and borne away by a great love for the girl on one hand, and dreading his father's opposition on the other, he had married her clandestinely, and had now brought her with him to Scotland, trusting that her beauty, sweetness, grace and virtue would open the heart of his father to them both, and pardon the fact of his having had, as he would have phrased it, a 'stolen march made upon him.'

The homeward journey had been but a portion of their honeymoon tour, and safe in her young husband's love, the girl seemed to see only a brilliant and happy, if somewhat vague, future. Aware of his father's temper, spirit, and infatuated pride of family, young Piers was not without some genuine anxiety as to the result, when the issue of his rashness seemed so close at hand.

'If your father is so proud as you say, Piers,' said the young wife—still a bride— as she nestled her sweet face in his neck, and his arm went caressingly round her, 'and if he will not forgive the *mésalliance* you have made with poor me——'

'Well, my darling, what then?'

'You may repent it,' said she, her dark eyes filling with tears, and her voice trembling with anxiety.

'Never, my own little wife—never! and by this time to-morrow I hope to see you taking your place at his table, as the future mistress of Eaglescraig; though long may the time be ere you are so, for my father is a dear old fellow—twice my age, at all events!'

The girl sighed softly, and hoped that all might be as they wished it.

'Welcome back, my boy!' exclaimed Sir Piers next day, when his son appeared (but alone) at Eaglescraig; 'why have you been so long in writing me? Why do you come thus suddenly? and *where* is your baggage? But how well you are looking; and, by Jove, you have a beard like a Brahmin!'

'I have a long story to tell you, sir, about all my adventures: one in particular, that may take some time to tell——'

'Then keep it till after dinner: let us have it with the Chateau Margaux,' said Sir Piers, laughing; and being timidly willing to delay till the last moment the revelation that was *inevitable,* his son—even with the sweet face of her who, at that moment, was alone in his memory—was glad of the little reprieve.

Anxious to make a good impression, he made a more than usually careful toilette in his own old and familiar room ; but when he took his seat at table, the presence of Tunley and the servants, and also of John Balderstone, who had dropped in on business, and whom the baronet had pressed to remain, precluded all reference to his secret for a time, till the cloth was removed, the dessert laid, the decanters ranged in rank-entire before the host, and Tunley was told he might withdraw till rung for.

'And now for your story, Piers,' said the elder Montgomerie ; 'the claret stands with you.'

'I must first drink to you, and congratulate you on your promotion,' replied his son.

'Yes, I am full colonel now, Piers, and may fairly hope to be a lieutenant-general some of these days. But now for the story,' he repeated uneasily ; 'I suppose John Balderstone may hear it ?'

'Of course, sir,' said Piers, coughing nervously, and twice draining his large green claret-glass to gain time, while he felt that his colour came and went, and his father's keen eyes were fixed upon him with equal scrutiny and affection.

Young Piers glanced at the stately table, with its massive plate, glittering crystal, rich wines and luxuriant fruit, and thinking with joy of her who would be the presiding goddess there to-morrow, told his narrative in a manly and honest manner, yet not without some trepidation of tone, while his father sat bolt upright in his chair, staring at him with a face expressive of rage, incredulity, and absolute grief, as if he felt that his only son and heir had gone mad. Worthy John Balderstone also looked scared and bewildered.

'And now, sir,' continued the son, despite the terrible frown that deepened on his father's face, 'I have told you all, except my darling's name.'

'Her name be —— ! what is her name to me ? Zounds, sir ! I don't want to hear it

—the daughter of a beggarly painter—an adventuress—to become in time Lady Montgomerie of Eaglescraig! No, sir, no; damme, I'll break the entail; I'll—I'll——'

Sir Piers for a few moments was literally choking with rage.

'That my wife is poor and nameless, according to your mode of thinking, father, is no fault of hers; her beauty is great, her goodness and accomplishments are rarely surpassed, and surely you will forgive us, we love each other so?' urged young Piers; and as he spoke his heart was in his voice, and his very soul seemed welling out of his fine dark eyes.

'May the moment that I forgive you and her be my last on earth!' thundered Sir Piers, smiting the table with his clenched hand; 'forgive you — not if I lived for a thousand years! Away—away! quit my sight and never let me see your face again!'

And literally he began to tutor himself to hate his son as much as he had idolised him before.

The latter rose from his chair; his handsome face seemed as if petrified—turned to stone, and with the colour of stone, his nether lip began to quiver painfully, for he too had a heart of fiery pride.

Sir Piers rang the bell so furiously that he nearly rent the wires.

'What are you about to do, sir?' asked his son.

'I am about to expel you from this house for ever!' replied Sir Piers. 'Order the waggonette which brought Mr. Montgomerie from his hotel round from the stables instantly,' he added to the astonished Tunley, whom the fierce summons —the bell was vibrating still—had brought up like a genius of the lamp; 'never again is he to set foot in the house which he has disgraced!'

In vain did worthy John Balderstone attempt to act the peace-maker; he was silenced by an imperious wave of the hand.

'This vile adventuress, for I am sure she is such, shall not quite gain her ends. I shall break the entail, if I can !' exclaimed Sir Piers, with growing exasperation ; 'by the God that hears me, I will !'

'Father, see her once — only once —ere you judge of her so cruelly ! And, oh ! let us not part thus ! One day you may repent it,' urged his son piteously, and yet not without some anger in his heart.

'Repent it ? never !' replied his father, with a wild and bitter laugh. 'Now then, Tunley, *is* that waggonette at the door ?'

'Yes, sir,' replied the butler, again appearing, and very much scared.

'Go !' said Sir Piers to his son ; 'as God is our judge, here for ever ends all between us !'

He turned and left the room by one door, while his son quitted it by another, and from that moment the father and son met no more. The latter's allowance was cut off ; he got into debt, sold his commission, and with his young wife eventually disappeared. Mr. Balderstone was supposed to be cognisant of his movements for a time under a false name ; however, the general never inquired, and after a year or so all traces of him were lost.

Proud of his ancient race, incapable personally of a dishonourable thought or guilty plan, his son's rash marriage, without his consent, and with an obscure girl, filled his heart with a species of black fury, and gave his face a look of repellent pride that was long its settled expression.

The fate of Piers became a kind of mystery—hidden ; though it is the fate of things in this world that, as a general rule, nothing is hid for ever.

There came a night which the general never forgot ! It was the night of an event which he related only to John Balderstone and one or two others, confidential friends, who were now no longer in the land of the living.

On the night referred to, the lonely general, then creeping up the vale of years, was seated in the library, lingering over his last glass of grog, and gazing, as

we last left him, into the glowing embers ;
his thoughts wandered away from present
things to the past in spite of himself. He
reviewed the things of old—forgotten say-
ings and doings in camp and quarters, in
the field and the Indian jungle ; the faces
and the voices of the distant and the dead
came back to him, and among them, more
powerfully than usual, the face and voice
of his lost son, Piers.

There was no sound in the room but the
steady and monotonous ticking of a great
antique clock on the black marble mantelpiece, and the snoring of a Highland stag-
hound stretched upon a deerskin before the
fire, unless we add that the night wind
moaned shudderingly through a coppice of
red-stemmed Scottish firs, and the beech-
trees swayed drearily in the passing
blast.

A sudden sense of some one being near
him—something intangible, too—came
over him ; he seemed to hear a sigh, and
brave though he was, his heart felt as if
dying within him, and the hair of his head

stood up, or a prickly sensation pervaded all his scalp.

Beside his chair a kind of shadow seemed to form itself, and become, with each pulsation of his pulses, more distinct in outline, till the face and form of his son were before him—the former wasted and pallid, his eyes full of sorrow and reproach. His hands seemed unusually white, wan, and the articulations of the fingers were painfully distinct, as those of one who had been wasted by fever, toil, and want.

A thousand maddening and terrifying thoughts seemed to whirl through the general's brain. He strove to start from his chair, but remained in it as if spellbound; he strove to cry aloud, but his voice failed him, or the faint sound he did utter seemed unnatural, and filled him with greater fear.

For a moment or two the upbraiding spirit, if spirit it was, or a creation of his own fevered fancy, stood before him, and then slowly melted away.

Sir Piers started to his feet.

'I have been dreaming,' he said, with a kind of gasping sigh. 'A plague on such dreams and fancies!'

But something seemed to tell him it was *not* a dream, and not a fancy, and he remembered that in the pale and wasted hands of the figure were a sheaf of small brushes such as artists use, and a mahlstick. Had Piers in his dire necessity betaken himself to art to gain a livelihood?

He sat for some time waiting and watching, in a state of awe, terror, and intense anxiety, for the appearance to return, but it came no more; but from that moment an assurance stole into his heart that his son must be dead—that he perhaps died at that particular moment: and then he began to think, and think, and think again, how hard and pitiless he had been; and his handsome face grew older and more lined, and wrinkles seemed to come where none were formed as yet. He might have said with Balder:

'I have lived in the past,
As by a deathbed, with unwonted love,
And much forgiveness as we bring to those
Who can offend no more.'

So time passed on, and old age came upon him—a childless old age.

His son was gone—he had no doubt of that! He had no nephew, no cousin, or cousin's son, to succeed him in the lands that had been in his family since the wars of Bruce and Wallace—yea, since Norwegian Haco's banner fell on the field of Largs ; and he began to fear that his title would become extinct, when, in the 'Landed Gentry of Grat Britain and Irelan d,' he found that Sir Bernard Burke had assigned a place to a certain Mr. Hew Montgomerie, then broiling in the Indian Civil Service, proving that he was the nearest living relative of the line of Eaglescraig.

His lawyers speedily communicated with that amiable personage, whom we have already introduced to the reader, and thus it is that he came to be resident at Eagles-

craig as heir of entail, and to the baronetcy.

The poor old general strove his hardest
to like Hew, who also strove sedulously,
and pretty skilfully, to keep his many bad
qualities secret from him; but often when
Sir Piers was in his thoughtful or sad
moods, he would ask Mary to sing to him
certain old songs that were associated in
some way with the long-lost Piers, and as
her soft voice went to the old man's heart,
and her pretty hands strayed over the
piano-keys, she 'soothed him to peace,' as
Mrs. Garth was wont to say, 'as the harp
of David had soothed King Saul with the
holy spell of sweet music;' but it was a
spell that always sent the thoughts of Sir
Piers to wander in Shadow-land.

CHAPTER XIV.

LESLIE FOTHERINGHAME.

'WELCOME back to Dumbarton, where I have been somewhat rather of a hermit since you left it—welcome back to pipeclay and all the "pomp, pride, and circumstance of glorious war!" The decanter is beside you, and I think there are some prime havannas left in that box. So, now, let us be jolly,' exclaimed Leslie Fotheringhame, as Falconer seated himself in the quarters of the former, a curious-looking, old-fashioned room—the same that had been occupied by the little Queen Mary in her twelfth year (ere she sailed to France, after the battle of Pinkie)—one of the oldest parts of the castle.

Falconer cast himself with an air of weariness into an easy-chair, though his journey from Eaglescraig had not been a very long one.

'What about our fellows, Fothering-hame?' he asked, manipulating a cigar.

'The detachment?'

'Yes.'

'There is not much to report; two fellows are in "the shop" for absence from parade; one in the cells, for being drunk and disorderly.; and little Fuddie, the drummer, has cut his stick—or sticks, should I say? Probably finding, as Sterne has it, that "the honour of beating a drum was likely to be its own reward," he has taken French leave and bolted. If caught, we should duck the fellow in the Clyde, but for the seventh clause of the sixth section on "Discipline," which prevents the adoption of punishments in detach-ments that are at variance with those in use at headquarters.'

Falconer continued to smoke in silence, so Fotheringhame spoke again.

'England expects every man to do his duty—but as cheaply as possible—for next to nothing, in fact; so, after your late surroundings, the luxury of my quarters will fail to impress you as either being useful or ornamental—as a certain poem has it, here are—

> ' "Apparatus for washing: a pail and a can,
> Part of an Army List, half of a fan,
> A fawn-coloured glove, a lock of false hair—
> Both highly prized gifts from some lady fair;
> A case of blunt razors, a shako and plume;
> A fishing-rod, shot-belt, rifle, and broom;
> An invite to dinner, the card of a priest,
> A sketch of the colonel described as 'a beast.' " '

While Fotheringhame ran on laughingly thus, Falconer was silent and pre-occupied, or replied only by a faint smile.

Leslie Fotheringhame was a handsome man, but of a different type from Cecil Falconer. He was taller and more squarely built, with deep-set and grave dark-blue eyes, the expression of which generally belied his merry manner; he was dark-haired, with a firm mouth, a clear dark skin and ponderous black moustache. His manner was ever honest, frank, and pleasant; and though his turn of mind was somewhat cynical—as if he had met with some disappointment in life—his face at times wore a smile that lit it up like a sunbeam.

Though junior to Cecil Falconer in the regiment, he was his senior by some years; for he had once been a captain of Lancers, but sold his troop, no one knew why, and afterwards obtained a non-purchase commission in the Cameronians. He was also greatly Cecil's senior in experience. He was wont to boast that he had, by a fluke, escaped the perilous meshes of matrimony, though the mess rather opined that he had been disappointed, 'thrown over,' by some girl, though none exactly knew the story.

'What is doing at headquarters?' asked Falconer.

'Birkie of that Ilk has sent in his papers.'

'Birkie—why?'

'Lost a pot of money on a hurdle-race at Streatham—it's a step in the regiment ; but everyone is very sorry for poor Birkie. Acharn has got into a scrape with a widow, whose husband suddenly turned up, so he has gone on leave, to be out of the way, and Freeport too.'

'Freeport—what was Dick up to ?'

'He proposed to three sisters in one night—all the daughters of a commandant of one of those confounded brigade depôts, and hearing that the adjutant might be sent for his sword, Dick was off like a bird by an early train for London. But we all know that Dick has an engagement-ring with a blue stone, which he gives to some girl everywhere, yet contrives to get back in a lover's quarrel when the route comes.'

To Fotheringhame it was apparent that his friend had come back to Dumbarton in a somewhat taciturn mood—cloudy in face and abstracted in manner.

'What the dickens has happened ?' thought he.

'Was our colonel—the old general—kind?' he asked.

'Very,' was the curt reply.

'And the ladies—kinder still, I suppose?' hazarded Fotheringhame, lying back in his chair and shooting concentric rings of tobacco-smoke upward. 'No answer—eh? Now, apropos of the subject of your remarkable letter, I hope that you have left Eaglescraig without committing yourself?'

'I played no more with that fellow Hew.'

'I am not thinking of Hew.'

'Committing myself—how?'

'By a proposal.'

'What had I to offer a girl so rich as Mary Montgomerie—an heiress, in fact?'

'All that a girl wants in a husband, I suppose—a deuced good-looking and presentable fellow of his inches.'

'I could never sink to be a dependent on my wife, Leslie. Had Mary been penniless——'

'Oh, come—we have got the length of calling her Mary, have we?'

'Had she been so, I might not have shrunk from asking her to share my poverty—for such it is; but her fortune is an impassable barrier between us—and I would to heaven that I had never set foot in Eaglescraig!'

'This is rather Quixotic,' said Fotheringhame, sipping his brandy and water, and humming—

'"'Tis madness to remember—'twere better to forget."'

'Moreover, if she marries without her guardian's consent, " then in that case," as the will has it, her money passes from her.'

'You seem to have had all the details through hand,' said Fotheringhame, drily.

'Not with her, at all events.'

'And she is attractive?'

'Attractive. is not the word—she is downright lovely, and good as she is lovely! But her guardian, the general, has decided on plans for her future.'

'A peerage?'

'Not at all. He resolves that she shall

marry the cub called Hew Montgomerie, who is the heir of entail—a kind of distant cousin.'

' Does—Mary affect him ?' asked Fotheringhame, with a quizzical smile.

' Not at all !   But I cannot tell you how much she has bewitched me.'

' Aware all the while of the plan in store for her.'

' I know what a sceptic you are about women, Leslie ; but her face is ever before me, by day and night.   I can see it now looking at me, out of that blank barrack wall, as plainly as I see yours.   She has indeed bewitched me !"

Fotheringhame looked at the wall indicated, shrugged his shoulders, and said, with a provoking laugh :

' I can't help thinking, old fellow, that the girl has been amusing herself with you, from the details you give me, and that a flirtation was all she wanted.'

' Fotheringhame !'

' Don't get excited.   I am sure that, like other dear creatures,

'Her feet are so very little,
　Her hands are so very white ;
Her jewels are so very heavy,
　Her head so very light ;
Her colour is made of cosmetics,
　Though this she never will own ;
Her body's made mostly of cotton,
　Her heart is made wholly of stone.'

'This may apply to some goddess of yours,' said Falconer, becoming seriously ruffled ; 'but as for me——'

'There will be no more larks or rows,' continued Fotheringhame, laughing ; 'no more chance medley flirtations at picnics or lawn tennis, or even in the conservatory ; our mind, or what is left of it, must run only on one ideal, and on presents of dainty gloves for lovely little hands, books and bouquets, chains, lockets, and bracelets, pressure of the taper fingers, perhaps even a chaste kiss, as Byron has it——'

'By Jove, Leslie, how you *can* gabble !' said Falconer, but without a smile, for something peculiarly uncomfortable and damping in the closing details of his visit to Eaglescraig haunted him.

Perceiving this, Fotheringhame's banter ceased, and after a pause he said :

'Pardon me, Cecil, if my jokes annoy you ; but if she does not wish to marry this fellow Hew, why should she ?'

' Why ?'

'Yes ; no power can compel her. The day is passed when girls can be married against their will, except in novels. There may be, I am aware, a mild system of domestic pressure, a steady and persevering domestic tyranny, quite as mischievous in the end, sometimes, as the brute force of the terrible old baron or stern parent of the Middle Ages ; and I have even known more than one case in which the feeble opposition of a girl has been foiled under the powerful home-current, as it flowed on and bore her away with it.'

' By Jove, Leslie, you *are* a Job's comforter ! And now, by-the-bye, there is another girl at Eaglescraig of whom I have not yet spoken—a lady on a visit.'

' And your mind was divided between them ?'

'Not at all, though the beauty and style of Annabelle Erroll are indescribable.'

'*Who* did you say?' exclaimed Leslie Fotheringhame, as his voice and face changed curiously, he took the cigar from his lips and sat bolt upright in his chair.

'Annabelle Erroll; she knows *you*, by the way, and I hope the general will, in turn, invite you to Eaglescraig.'

'I hope not,' said Fotheringhame, sadly and fervently; 'by Jove, I hope not!'

'Why?'

'Why? Because I would not go under any circumstances or pressure, from what you tell me.'

'As to what, or whom? Hew Montgomerie?'

'Hew be hanged! No.'

'Who then?'

'Annabelle Erroll,' said Fotheringhame, uttering the name sadly, softly, and with unction.

'So, thereby hangs a tale.'

'Yes, old fellow—a devil of a tale I would rather not unfold.'

'Then you have had your little weakness too ?'

'Of course ; I've been in love like other —fools ; who has not ?'

Cecil Falconer, however, was too full of his own affair to ponder long over the mysterious intimacy that existed, or had existed, between Annabelle Erroll and Leslie Fotheringhame.

CHAPTER XV.

SEPARATED.

THOUGH grievously disappointed that his late guest should have proved the gamester Hew described him to be, and not ill-pleased to have a rival of the latter at a distance from Eaglescraig, Sir Piers, to do him justice, in the kindness of his heart, missed his friend, the genial young officer, who had been so patient a listener to those dreary Indian reminiscences, over which Hew openly groaned and secretly swore.

Mrs. Garth and Annabelle Erroll missed him for his musical accomplishments and conversational qualities, and poor Mary missed him more than all, while her aversion to Hew became more undisguised than ever, and he spitefully retorted by saying more than once in her hearing that ' a deuced good lesson had been taught Sir Piers never again to invite, without a due and accredited introduction, any chance-medley fellow to Eaglescraig.'

Her manner to his heir at last drew upon her the animadversion of Sir Piers.

' My dear girl,' said he to her one day, ' I must remonstrate with you, as the betrothed wife of Hew.'

' Betrothed ! by whom ?' asked Mary, with mingled gravity and anger.

' By me, my darling ; as such, I say, you owe him some duty, and some respect, and a deference to his opinions. School yourself to love him properly in the time to come, and not distress your poor old grand-uncle and guardian, who loves you so well for your dead parents' sake.'

' I do not, and cannot love him !' said the girl, wearily.

'Not now, you think; but in time, Mary, in the good time to come,' he continued, stroking her rich, dark hair caressingly, as if she were yet a little child; and when he adopted a pleading tone and manner, rather than those of authority and command, she felt a deeper emotion of pain and annoyance.

'There is no necessity for having romantic notions, or being desperately fond of your intended husband. The notions and the love will come in due time after marriage,' said the old man, who had well-nigh forgotten all about his own early love and marriage, which had come to pass so long ago. 'You have wealth, Mary.'

'What is wealth, if linked with unhappiness?'

'Hew will make you a good husband; if he did not—if he did not!' and the general paused, and grasping the knob of his arm-chair, looked unutterable things at the idea of such a contingency. 'As I have said a hundred times since he

came from India, with your fortune added
to what I shall leave—all going to Hew
as heir of entail—the future baronet of
Eaglescraig will, in wealth, be second to
none, richer by far than half the peerage ;
and marry you cannot, without my permission.'

'But to marry when one cannot love is
—is——'

'What, girl ?' asked Sir Piers, peevishly,
for he had not again referred to the suspected fancy for Cecil Falconer, though
his mind was full of it.

'Falsehood and dishonesty, rank injustice,
and shameful !'

'Well—anything more ?' he continued
angrily.

'Yes—destruction of soul and body,
perhaps.'

'Mary, you do not look beyond the
present,' said Sir Piers, with growing
sternness, to find his pet scheme so
vigorously opposed ; 'hence it is my im-
perative duty to do that for you, and with

a firm will and resolute hand to scheme out a happy future.'

'How miserably had he schemed out the future of his poor dead son!' thought Mrs. Garth, as she led Mary away in tears and anger.

Meanwhile, if Hew looked upon himself as the future lord and master of Mary Montgomerie and her thousands, still more surely did he look upon himself as the future laird, lord, and master of Eaglescraig and all that appertained thereto; and while impatiently looking forward to the day of his succession, gave himself, unknown to Sir Piers, such airs with old and valued adherents, such as John Balderstone the factor, Tunley the aged butler, whose taste in wine he scouted; Pate Pastern the head groom, who was cognisant of some of his tricks on the turf; old Sandy Swanshott the head keeper, with even Mrs. Garth and others, that, certes, he won anything but golden opinions from all !

Between him and John Balderstone

there was a species of smouldering feud.
The latter loved and revered Sir Piers,
and always winced when Hew showed, as
he had the coarseness and ill-feeling to do,
that he actually prayed for the sudden or
premature arrival of the time when he
should figure as Sir Hew Montgomerie ;
premature it could scarcely be now, though
the hale old man seemed to have years of
life in him yet.

Mr. Balderstone was not slow in perceiving how Hew disliked their late visitor,
Cecil Falconer, and thus was disposed to
vaunt his praises in the mere spirit of
opposition.

'I can't perceive the fellows' merits in
any way,' growled Hew with an oath,
as they entered the smoking-room one
evening.

'That I can very well believe,' replied
the old gentleman, drily.

'How—why ?' demanded Hew, suspect-
ing something in his tone.

'Plainly, then, to do so would argue the
existence of what you do not possess.'

'What is that—perception?'

'No.'

'What then?'

'Some refinement of taste,' replied Mr. Balderstone, his dark grey eyes beaming as he made a home-thrust, for which Hew quickly revenged himself in a fashion of his own, causing the portly Mr. Balderstone, as he seated himself, to spring up with a malediction.

'What the devil is the row?' asked Hew.

'Only this, sir, that you have placed a pair of sharp jack-spurs upon the chair you so politely accorded me!'

'And you have a sanguinary sense of sitting down on the rowels — eh?' said Hew, laughing heartily, and not even attempting an apology, while his shifty eyes now beamed with delight.

'I presume these spurs are a present to you, from your friend Mr. Welsher Twigg, the gentleman rider, whose peculiar riding so favoured you at Ayr and York last year,' said Mr. Balderstone, with some

contempt of manner, while Hew's parti-
coloured eyes now gleamed with rage, for it
was averred on the turf, that bribed by him,
the rider in question, when pretending to
give a horse a bucket of water, daubed his
nostrils with blood, to make people believe
the animal had broken a bloodvessel, and
had secretly loosened the nails in the shoes
of another, at a hurdle-race, to prevent him
winning.

As these black rumours had never
reached the ear of Sir Piers, Mr. Balderstone felt that he had 'scored one' by the
taunt; but in a time to come, and by both
unforeseen then, he was to run up a terrible
and crushing score against Hew Montgomerie, with a result that neither could
have imagined.

Slowly passed the days now with Mary.
The spacious house was full of new guests,
and pleasant ones too, but it seemed dull
and dreary, since *he* was no longer there.
His place was vacant. The click of balls
came from the billiard-room, and the sound
of merry voices, but his was no longer

there, or at her piano now. All seemed changed to Mary. Sir Piers never adverted to his visit, his name or his existence ; and scarcely ever to the old and invariable topic of the Cameronians.

Why was this ? Did he suspect their secret, or was Hew the spirit of evil ? She could not doubt that ; and her sympathetic friend Annabelle Erroll, who was a close observer of affairs, and had all Mary's confidence, thought so too.

But Annabelle Erroll had thoughts that were peculiarly her own, over the departure of Cecil Falconer.

'He has gone from me to Leslie,' she said to herself; 'to Leslie Fotheringhame, to tell him that he has spent a whole month with me—a month in my society, and I have given no sign that Leslie's existence was ever aught to me—at least, I hope so—and yet there was a time when I was all the world to him ! Yes—yes— it is indeed over and done with, the love that was once ours. Will Leslie ask him how I am looking ?' (she glanced at her soft

blonde beauty in the mirror). 'Or how I
am comporting myself—sadly or merrily?—
if I am unchanged from the Annabelle of
the time that can come no more?'

For some mysterious reason she had not
taken her friend Mary into her confidence
at first, when Fotheringhame's name was
spoken of; and now she shrunk from doing
so, lest she might seem wanting in candour;
and, as the love she referred to was 'over
and done with,' what mattered it now?

And yet often Mary might have drawn
such a confidence from her.

'Oh, Annabelle,' she would sometimes
say, 'so quick is fancy, that occasions there
are when I see a figure like Cecil's in the
distance—the figure of some one else, whose
walk or gesture recalls him vividly to me—
that I feel something like a sharp pang in
my heart.'

As days passed on and became weeks,
Mary's movements and manner became
languid, and all her old occupations, if not
neglected, were pursued with a weary
indifference. She had lost interest even in

being dressed to perfection, as she had always been, and spent hours in the seclusion of her own room, or exclusively in the society of Annabelle Erroll.

Her eyes lost their clear brilliance and became heavy in expression; her usually gentle and playful manner was changed for petulance and irritability, all signs of where and how her thoughts were—signs which Hew watched with jealous rage, and loving, old Sir Piers with unaffected solicitude, mingled with bitterness at Falconer, and at himself for that which he now deemed his own fantastic idea of *camaraderie* and old military hospitality.

'Never again,' he would mutter to himself, 'never again will I play the fool! Hew is right—Hew is right!'

His pet from her orphan childhood, his artless, father-like experience of her, had, until quite recently, prevented him from remarking that she was no longer a baby-faced girl, but a grown woman—a bird that might leave him for another nest—and then a kind of nervous thrill went through his heart, when he thought a love for another might take possession of her; and thus he became doubly anxious to secure her for Hew.

'How pale and ill you look, my darling!' said Mrs. Garth to her, at the close of a day that had seemed a long and dreary one to Mary.

'What matters it?' said she, petulantly; 'Cecil cannot see me now,' she added mentally, as her eyes wandered through the window to the wooded walk that led to the grotto—the grotto where Cecil had first told her of his love, and where his lips had touched hers for the first and last time, and the host of tender recollections that hallowed the place flowed full upon her memory. 'Why are some people sent into this world only to be miserable!' sighed the lovely heiress, while surrounded by every luxury that world could furnish. 'I wonder if we ever lived before and were happy—or if we shall live again, and be happier still! Who can tell—who knows?'

Then tenderly and fondly she recalled the words of Cecil, when he spoke to her of the mysterious sympathy that, in his solitary moments, had seemed to link his soul, or existence, with that of another, and could she doubt now that it was her own!

And with this idea, a tender and loving expression would steal over her delicate *mignonne* face.

'Rouse yourself, my darling,' Mrs. Garth would say, 'ride or drive—read or work.'

'Read—read! I hate books now—I hate crewel-work, music, everything!' she replied, almost snappishly; 'dear old Garthy, I am no longer a schoolgirl, and I never, at any time, was one cut to the Hannah More pattern.'

She had learned from his own lips how Cecil loved her; but now Cecil was gone and never could return, and all her little world seemed sunless and cold—dark and desolate. She was no longer alternately amused and petulant, coquettish and light-hearted, for a settled moodiness had come

over her—the gloom of sorrow, not anger;
and though no one, not even Annabelle,
surprised her in tears, her eyes sometimes
bore unmistakable traces of recent weep-
ing.

A wild longing would, at times, come
over her to see Cecil again—to hear his
voice—to know what he was doing, or with
whom he was at that particular moment;
but the days passed vaguely and drearily
on, while she thought of him, dreamt of
him, talked in fancy to him, and wove such
romances about him and herself, as only a
young girl can weave.

He was not very distant from her after
all, and yet he might, so far as their inter-
course was concerned, have been at the
Antipodes; for no tidings, no news of him,
ever came to Eaglescraig, and at last, to
Mary, it began to seem as if the sweet
bright chapter in her life, about Cecil
Falconer, was utterly ended!

And probably she would never love
again, she thought; for that she had given
him was the one love of a lifetime.

But the general and Mrs. Garth thought they knew better; and that her ailment was only a girlish fancy, that naturally would pass away and be forgotten.

CHAPTER XVI.

ANNABELLE ERROLL.

NOW Leslie Fotheringhame, though disposed at first to be somewhat reticent on the subject of his previous intimacy with Annabelle Erroll, after a time confided their mutual story to Cecil Falconer.

Thrown together as he and the latter were, in that lonely and isolated fort, the whole garrison of which, besides their own detachment, consisted only of a master gunner and a few old pensioners, it was natural that they should have their mutual confidences over their after-dinner cigars, and thus Falconer heard all about it from Fotheringhame.

'You see, old fellow, it came to pass in this way.

'My troop of Lancers was quartered in Perth Barracks, while the head-quarters were stationed at Piershill. I soon tired of all the little gaieties afforded by the Fair City; but the season was summer, and the Tay afforded me endless amusement for fly-fishing and boating; and, as one of my subs was on leave and the other on the sick-list, I was somewhat thrown on my own resources.

'I had a swift light shallop, in which I used to pull daily, when the tide or stream served, from the bridge upward past the wooded slopes of Kinnoull, and away for miles amid the loveliest and most luxuriant sylvan scenery in the world.

'One day the heat was very great, and, ceasing to row, I lay back in the stern-sheets of my boat, with a cigar between my lips, and let her float, lazily, on the current of the stream, which flowed between its wooded banks deeply, silently, and majestically. On every hand around me

were a long series of varied hills covered
with picturesque foliage of every shade of
green, the vista everywhere terminated by
the more remote mountains, the rich tints
of which were softened in the blue haze
and by the distance.

'At a bend of the river my boat partially grounded, but I felt too lazy to shove
off, and lay there under the shadows cast
upon the bright stream by the overreaching
elms, oaks, and silver birches, among the
blended foliage of which the blue doves
were cooing, and where the wild violets and
jasmine grew close to the water's-edge.
On all the river I thought there could be
no lovelier spot than this. Save the still-
ness of its flow, and the hum of the mountain honey-bee among the wild flowers of
the wood, in and out of the gueldre-roses
and foxglove-bells, there was no sound in
the air, as I lay there in a kind of day-
dream, with my arms resting idly on my
sculls, till the voice of a girl, singing close
by, roused me at once to attention.

'Sweetly she sung, and seemed to give

her whole soul and pathos to the song. She thought no ear save her own was within hearing; but for a time the singer remained unseen by me.

> ' " ' Love me always—love me ever,'
> Said a voice low, sad, and sweet;
> ' Love me always—love me ever,'
> Memory will the words repeat."

' And in truth, Falconer, I give them by an effort of memory now, it is so long since I heard and read them:

> ' " While in fancy still beside me,
> Is her fair and graceful form;
> And I hear the murmured love-words,
> Gushing from her heart so warm.

> ' " From her heart, subdued by sorrow,
> In its fond and trusting youth,
> Till she trembles lest the morrow
> Rob some idol of its—truth?"

' A slight impetus which I gave my boat with one of the sculls, brought me quite suddenly to the very feet of the singer, as she stood on the edge of the stream, embowered among foliage, and shaded by the light aspen-like sprays of the silver birches, regarding me with some surprise, for my boating costume, I dare say, was novel in that quarter, and seeming irresolute as to whether she should retire—any way, advance she could not.

' I saw at a glance that the girl was just at that age which is between childhood and maidenhood, that she was perfectly lady-like, delicate in form and figure, and possessed of rare beauty of the fairest, or blonde type; her hair of the lightest brown, and shot with gold that made it brilliant in the flakes of sunlight that flashed between the trees; her eyes, of dark-grey blue, had brows and lashes so dark as to impart great character to her otherwise soft and *mignonne* face; but you know well who I am describing.

' She had a bunch of wild-flowers in one hand; the other grasped the ribbons of her tiny hat, which she was swinging to and fro, as she had come through the wood bareheaded, and was evidently not far from her home.

' " Pardon me," said I, lifting my cap,

"but I am afraid that I am rather a tres-
passer here."

' " Not at all, sir; the river is free to
everyone."

' " But I have been almost ashore, and is
not that presuming too far ?" I asked again,
only for the pleasure of conversing with
her.

' " Oh no," she replied, with a charming
smile.

' " But I have disturbed you, I fear."

' " How ?"

' " I heard you singing—need I say, how
sweetly !"

' " An old song, quoted from some old
book, but the melody far surpasses the
words."

' " Yes, as sung by your voice," said I,
gallantly.

' " What a pretty boat yours is ! Have
you rowed far ?"

' " All the way from the bridge."

' " You must be weary, otherwise I
would ask you——"

' She blushed and paused.

' "I am not at all weary, and am every way at your service."

' " Oh, thanks ; will you row to the other side, and bring me some of the lovely——"

' She mentioned some peculiar kind of fern.

' " Permit me to row you across, and you can select them for yourself."

' Her eyes sparkled with pleasure, but she hesitated.

' "You mistrust a stranger," said I; "and perhaps your papa might be displeased——"

' "Poor papa is dead; but mamma would, I know, be angry. She is full of strict and strange notions; thus I can never venture far alone."

' " But the distance is so short——"

' " And she is always busy at this hour."

' "Come, then."

' She confidingly put her little hand in mine, sprang with charming grace lightly into the cushioned seat astern, and exclaimed with girlish delight:

' "What a lovely boat! How delicious

16—2

this is! Though we live only a mile from the Tay, I have never had a row on it."

' "Permit me to give you a little one now," said I, assuming my sculls, and shot the boat out into mid-stream. I regarded her beauty with growing admiration and pleasure; but my Lancer experiences caused the thought to occur, could she be so innocent, so utterly guileless as she seemed?

'Some ferns were speedily selected, and uprooted by my knife, also some magnificent water-lilies from a pool under the trees; and, as she seemed thoroughly to enjoy herself upon the sunlit river, I pulled her to and fro, near the silver birches where I first met her, and she chatted away to me as if she had known me for months. That she was a lady in birth and breeding was indisputable; her accent was highly cultivated and her manners refined, and everything about the girl betokened gentle blood; but there was an artlessness combined with girlish abandon about her, that made me curiously and uncharitably suspicious, while deeply and suddenly in-

terested in her. Thus I said, after a pause,
while letting the boat drift with the current, and keeping the blades of my sculls
just out of the water:

' "You do me great honour, and must
have singular confidence in me, a stranger,
that you trust yourself with me thus."

' " How we glide !" exclaimed the girl,
with childish glee. "Oh, I could sail here
for ever !"

' "What would mamma think, if she
knew it ?"

' " Being with you ?"

' " Yes."

' " I scarcely know what she would think ;
but I know what she would *do*," was the
reply.

' "Admonish you ?"

' " Yes ; and lock me up for days to
come. But I can see, of course, that you
are a gentleman."

' " Thanks for the compliment."

' "But it is difficult to say what else ;
your costume is so unlike anyone we see
hereabout."

' I wore simply a rowing suit of white flannel, trimmed and faced with blue, with a skull-cap to match.

' " I am a Lancer," said I.

' " A Lancer !" she repeated, while her blue eyes dilated.

' " Yes ; I command the troop in Perth Barracks."

' I could see that the information pleased her, for her colour rose and she looked aside ; and again I pondered as to whether she was the hoyden by nature I suspected.

' " I must return home now," she said suddenly, as if she read my thoughts in my face.

' " So soon !" I urged, pleadingly.

' " Yes ; and thanks, so much, for your row—it has been delightful."

' " I shall be so glad to row you further next time."

' " You talk as if you expected to see me again—as if it were quite a matter of course."

' " I can only hope to do so," said I,

handing her ashore and retaining her little,
ungloved hand, lingeringly in mine ; " but I
row past here every day, *at the same hour.*"

' " Good-bye," said she, about to turn
away.

' " May I ask your name ?" said I, cap
in hand.

' " Annabelle Erroll."

' " Why do you start so ?" she asked
laughingly, and, tripping up the bank,
vanished among the white stems of the
silver birches, leaving her ferns in the boat
behind her.

' Start ! Well might I do so ; for I now
discovered that she was my cousin, the
daughter of a widowed maternal Aunt
Annabelle, with whom my parents had
ever been at enmity, about some money
quarrel, with her husband, Colonel Erroll—
an aunt whom I had never met, and of
whose existence I had but a vague idea.

' My cousin she was, and proud, greedy
old Uncle Erroll's daughter ! I would
rather not have heard this ; for the girl's
rare beauty attracted me powerfully on one

hand, while the transmitted stories of the family feud—stories which in boyhood made me regard the colonel and his wife as an ogre and ogress—on the other, had a fatal effect upon me.

'That her mother yet kept up the feud, was evident from the circumstance that she had never mentioned to Annabelle the fact, which she must have known, that I commanded the Lancers at the barrack within a few miles of their own house. Yet to have done so would have served no end; though I thought not of that.

'Would the young girl understand, or accept, my *hint?*

'When, on the following day, I betook me to the bend of the river in my boat, she was not there. I waited long, and reluctantly pulled away with a certain emotion of pique. But, on the *next* day again, at the same hour, I saw her light skirt flitting among the silver birches, and at once crept inshore. I had cut some fresh fern roots for her, in place of those she had forgotten.

'"Ah, how thoughtful and kind of you,"

she exclaimed, as she gave me her hand, and allowed me to lead her on board, quite as a matter of course.

' " You will have a little row to-day ?" said I.

' " A very tiny one it must be, then ; I am so afraid of mamma," she replied ; and in another minute we were skimming over the silvery water.

' " Have you mentioned to your mamma your meeting with me ?" I inquired.

' " With you—a stranger ? Oh, I dare not, Captain Fotheringhame."

' " You know my name, then !"

' " I saw in a newspaper, by the merest chance, that you were a guest of Lord Rothiemay's."

' For certain cogent reasons of my own, I could not help colouring like a great schoolboy at this peer's name, as I had been involved in something closer than a mere flirtation with a daughter of his ; but in the present instance, while feeling already inclined to be rather cousinly, I resolved to remain incog. as long as I could.

I knew that she would not mention my name at home, and so resolved to abandon myself to the perilous charm of her society during the absence of the Rothiemays in London. I admit freely that I was wrong, selfish in this, and severely was I punished in the end.

'This second day on the river was succeeded by many others, during which I gave myself completely up to the fascination of my new companion, who was so bright, quaint, and *spirituelle*, and full of enthusiasm for music, flowers, scenery, and everything, that she was unlike any other girl I had ever met—more than all, most unlike in style of beauty and manner the stately and patrician daughter of Rothiemay.

The boat, in the blaze of the sunshine, was drifting with the current; my sculls in the rowlocks rested on my knees; my cigar, the place and time, disposed me for luxurious reverie; and opposite me sat this beautiful girl, her hat beside her, her golden hair and fair face shaded by her parasol, while she sang in a low voice her song, "Love me always—love me ever," her eyes fixed dreamily on the wooded shore the while.

'" Annabelle," said I, softly.

'" Who gave you leave to call me by that name?" she asked, pouting.

'" Is it not your name?"

'" Yes, Captain Fotheringhame."

'" And a very pretty one; yet not even pretty enough for you. Why may I not call you by it?"

'" It sounds odd on your lips—already."

'" But not unpleasant, I hope?"

'She laughed, but became silent, and glanced at me shyly under her long lashes —shyly, and yet at times I thought half invitingly, half defiantly, too. Was the girl acting or not? I felt inclined to love her one moment, and simply and selfishly to amuse myself with her the next, heedless, perhaps, of whether the poor girl might learn to love me or not.

' I was a young fellow then, Falconer— save in experience, I am not an old fellow yet—but she was younger still, a very girl, on the borders between childhood and womanhood, the "sweet seventeen" of the inevitable love story. I was playing with fire, and so was she; and in teaching her to love me, I forgot all about an entanglement elsewhere, and gave myself up to the romance and intoxication of the time and the episode. So we met and dreamed on day by day, and she was so brilliantly happy that her soft face at times seemed to be singularly brightened by the very gladness of her heart; for it seems so natural for a young girl to mingle something of idolatry with her first love.

It did occur to me that our love—hers, at least—was somewhat of the rash and romantic Romeo and Juliet, passionate and unreasoning kind; while she was as young and innocent as I was exacting, and even suspicious that she was perfectly artless. I pondered over the words of Shakespeare: "Love sought is good; but given unsought is better;" and I was cynic, casuist, and egotist enough to doubt this.

' When I kissed her, it seemed each time

as if all my soul went out to her with that
kiss ; and yet—what idiosyncrasy of the
heart was it that made me wish to have
that kiss recalled !

' " I seem to have no wish or desire in
the world ungratified," she whispered to
me, as she nestled her head on my
shoulder, while the boat drifted with the
current under the tremulous shade of the
silver birches, and the Tay rippled placidly
past them.

' " You are so happy, Annabelle ?"

' " I never thought to be so happy as I
am now, Leslie ; I could even die with
your arms round me ! But—but are you
satisfied to have such an ignorant little girl
for your wife ?"

' *Wife !* I had not proposed yet ; and
the word roused me to a selfish consciousness of the rashness of the whole affair,
and so instead of replying I gave her a
tender caress, and said :

' " You are too good for me, Annabelle !"

' " I can scarcely believe it—you so
handsome, so rich—a captain of Lancers,

and all that! Oh, Leslie, God forbid you should ever cease to love me less than you do!"

'This crisis in my river-cruising roused me to think of what I was about; and still more was I roused when at the barracks I found a letter from Lord Rothiemay awaiting me with an invitation to spend a few days at his place. But to leave my troop then was impossible, thus I wrote thanking his lordship, and proposing simply to gallop over on an evening named to dinner, and as I despatched the missive, the face and figure of his daughter Blanche came reproachfully before me.

'I have already referred to an entanglement—it was simply that, though no promise had been given, I deemed myself all but engaged to Blanche Gordon, who, some months before this time had enchanted and spell-bound me. She was, indeed, a beautiful girl, and is a beautiful woman now, tall, slender, and graceful—a finished creature in every way, and wielding every natural and acquired accomplishment with consummate and yet unapparent art.

'She had given me every reason to believe that the passion with which she had inspired me was reciprocated, and we had only parted with the mutual hope, apparently, of meeting again; hence there seemed an absolute necessity for breaking off my philandering on the river. It is said that a man cannot love two women at once; and yet my heart ached for Annabelle and the grief that was before her.

'By some sophistry I nursed myself into the idea that I, rather than she, was the victim of circumstances; and as I went to the trysting-place for the last time I muttered :

'"'Handsome, rich, and a Lancer,'" she said. "Yes—yes, by Jove! she is not so deuced artless, after all; and the very proposal she made to me was in itself unwomanly."

'*Unwomanly!* I actually had the cruelty to tell her so ; and never shall I forget the look of incredulity, grief, dismay, and horror that appeared by turns, and then all blended together, in her beautiful face when I did so; and, already repenting what I had said so capriciously, I would have retracted my words if it were possible to do so.

'The phrase went through her loving heart like a bolt of ice, though she seemed to hear it indistinctly.

'"Oh, Leslie!" she gasped, in an accent of desolation such as human lips can utter but once in a lifetime, while her hands became cold and her face grew livid. She bit her lips till the blood came, and clasped her white hands until a ring I had given her marked her tender fingers; and then remembering it, she tore it off, cast it at my feet, and after giving me one long glance of anguish and reproval, tottered away home; and I, my heart burning with shame, shot my shallop out into the stream, and pulled away from the spot like a madman!

'"She is young, poor girl, and will get over it," thought I; while to nerve myself

I conjured up the presence of Blanche Gordon in all her imperial beauty, while, ingrate that I was! she that I had just left possessed and showed all the qualities that win love—and that love had, upon a mere pretence, been coldly and abruptly thrust back upon her heart.

'The black "morrow" of her prophetic song had come indeed, and an idol had been robbed of its truth.

'She was helpless to avenge herself, suffering and so beautiful; so I prayed that God might strengthen her, until some other love consoled her for the loss of mine; and even the thought of that stung me.

'"Yes, yes," thought I, "if so ready to love me, she will with equal facility learn to love another."

'There was no jealousy in the heart of Annabelle, for she knew nothing of any rival; but she was tormented by a sensation of loneliness and utter desolation by day and night, and disappointment was not the least element of that torment. But her time of vengeance was at hand.

'Next day saw me at Rothiemay, and at the feet, if I may say so, of Blanche Gordon, who received me with one of her usual bewitching smiles. My proposal certainly pleased and agitated her, but she told me with considerable confidence and coolness that she was engaged to another, and, indeed, was to be married in three weeks !

'The hollow damsel of fashion had thrown me over for a well-gilded coronet, just as I had thrown over—but coarsely and suspiciously—the girl who only loved me better than I deserved, and whose sweet society I now missed fearfully.

'But I was justly punished, you will say ; yet the story does not end here.

'Some weeks after, when family misfortunes came upon me, and I was compelled to sell out—to leave the Lancers—impelled I know not by what emotion or motive, unless it were something like force of habit and a restless craving, I roamed towards the old trysting-place, beneath the silver birches.

'Things of love and joy seldom repeat themselves, but my heart leaped on seeing Annabelle seated on the bank of the stream, half hidden by the wild rose-trees. Thither, no doubt, to torment her own heart, she had perhaps been in the habit of repairing to dream over the love that would never come again. She seemed lost in thought, and neither saw nor heard my approach ; and I saw the sunlight flashing on the bright, soft, golden hair, amid which my fingers had so often strayed.

' "Annabelle !" said I softly ; and she sprang up with a nervous start. "You see I am here again, to crave your pardon and to thank God that life has yet something worth living for—your love, Annabelle !"

' "And yours ?" she said disdainfully ; then her fortitude gave way, and for a moment she hid her burning face and her hot tears in her white and wasted hands, which, when I attempted to take them, repelled mine.

' "I will try to atone for the past, Annabelle—forgive me," said I, humbly.

' " I do forgive you," she replied with sudden calmness, grace, and a bearing of dignity I had never before seen in her; " but you can never be to me what you have been. You were the very idol of my heart, and with all my soul I worshipped you, Leslie; but that is ended now and for ever."

' " If a life of devotion, Annabelle——"

' " Say no more—I will not listen."

' " You decline my love, because ruin has come upon me at the hands of others, and I am compelled to leave the Lancers ?"

' Her eyes flashed, yet not with anger, and her bosom heaved, as she replied :

' " I grieve for what you say ; and God knows it is not so—but for the manner in which you reproached me with *unwomanly* conduct, that roused my proper pride. I did love you tenderly, purely, passionately, then ; but in repelling you, my conduct at least is womanly now ! Farewell then, for ever ; we leave this place to-morrow."

' " For where ?"

' "That can be a matter of no interest to you, Captain Fotheringhame," she replied, turning to retire.

' "Do not let us part thus, Annabelle. It is for your sake as much as my own that I sue thus."

' She crested up her little head haughtily.

' "Believe in my love," I urged.

' "I neither believe in it, nor want it— now at least."

' "How pitiless you are!" I exclaimed.

' "Just as you were ; so to part is best for us both. I once dreamt of being only too happy ; I am sadly awake now."

' Our eyes met for the last time : the expression of hers was passionless and decided. I had nothing to hope from her ; but I sighed deeply, with sorrow, pique, and even jealousy, as I watched her departing steps and saw the last flutter of her skirt between the stems of the silver birches, and then pulled slowly away from the trysting-place, never to seek it again !

' I can remember yet how the woods and lawns along the river's bank looked dreamily indistinct in the evening haze, as I pulled slowly and sadly homeward.

'Never since, till you spoke of her, have I heard aught of Annabelle Erroll, but I have since had reason to believe that she heard, in time, of my affair with Blanche Gordon.'

So all this story of Leslie Fothering-hame's was the secret so skilfully concealed under the calm exterior of the beautiful blonde whom Cecil Falconer had met at Eaglescraig.

CHAPTER XVII.

HOPES AND FEARS.

'THAT was the way our affair of the heart came about, and was ended by my pride, vacillation, and suspicion,' said Fotheringhame; 'and now I have little doubt that she is quite aware that I—the Lancer lover—was her cousin, though I never told her so.'

'How odd of you to act so!' exclaimed Cecil.

'Odd—I was mad, I think!'

'From her manner and words, I thought that you and she possessed in common some mysterious antecedents.'

'An unpleasant way of putting it,' said

Fotheringhame, with a shade of annoyance in his face; 'all that time was one of gloom to me. When I had to leave the Lancers I shall never forget the shock it gave me— though of course expected—to see the 'Army List' without my name in it; nor was I ever satisfied till I saw it there again, as a Cameronian. So you see, Falconer, that with all my general heedlessness of bearing, my life has not been without "its little romance, as most lives have, between the age of teetotum and tobacco," as George Eliot has it.'

'I may yet be the means of relighting this old flame again,' said Falconer; 'though it is said that there is nothing so difficult to revive as an old flirtation.'

'It was no flirtation——'

'Save in so far as you were concerned.'

'Until I lost Annabelle, I never knew how much I loved her, and how dear she was to me.'

'If Annabelle Erroll ever loved you she loves you still.'

'Why do you think so?'

' Because true love never dies,' said Falconer enthusiastically, for his mind was full of Mary's image; 'and I can now recall much that was strange in her mode and manner, if I mentioned you incidentally—of which I thought nothing then, but to which you have now given me a clue.'

' For all that you can tell, Falconer, she may only remember me with hatred, therefore it were better to forget the past and all about it. After confiding the matter to my two other friends—a quiet weed and M. de Cognac—I'll turn in, and so good-night.'

Most uneventfully passed the early days of spring, to Falconer, in the solitary castle of Dumbarton, which shoots up abruptly from a flat level, and stands completely isolated, the most prominent and picturesque object amid the beautiful scenery of the blue and majestic Clyde, into the channel of which it projects—a channel through the clear waters of which on a calm day, one may see whole forests of luxuriant seaweed, waving fathoms deep below.

Perched in the hollow or rift between the two great volcanic peaks into which this singular, mitre-shaped rock is cleft—the highest being five hundred and sixty feet in height—the old-fashioned barracks contain accommodation for only about a company of soldiers, and an ancient armoury (among the stores of which is the blade of Wallace's sword, fitted with a new hilt of a later period), and which is still identified as having been the prison of the Scottish Patriot, after his betrayal by the infamous Menteith. The circumstance of his sword having a hilt more modern than the blade, has led to its identity being doubted by those who are ignorant of the fact, that in the accounts of the Lord High Treasurer in 1505, we find mention made of the 'binding of Wallas's sword (in the castle of Dumbarton) with cords of silk and a *new hilt* and plomet (pommel), new skabbard and new belt to the said sword, xxvj sh.'

The entrance to the castle is by a barrier-gate at the foot of the rock and fronting the south east. It is defended by ramparts and guns, and immediately within it are the officers' quarters. A steep flight of stone steps gives access to the barracks, the well, and other batteries; from whence, and especially from Wallace's Seat—the highest peak of this stupendous rock—and the circular Roman tower, or fragment, perchance, of the days when Balclutha was the abode of Roderick Hael 'the Generous,' there is a glorious panorama of scenery: the far expanse of the Clyde, the sylvan vale of the Leven, the vast blue mass of Ben Lomond and the mountains of Arrochar, their peaks sometimes veiled in silvery mist.

On the giddy summit Falconer lingered for many an hour, and fancied he could see, more than twenty miles distant, as the crow flies, the hills that looked down upon Eaglescraig. There, when Fotheringhame was absent on some duty or pleasure, he smoked many a solitary havanna in solitude, in the evening and the gloaming, conversing in imagination with Mary Montgomerie, with a fond enthusiasm and a passion inflamed by obstacles and opposition, long after the shadows had deepened in the vale of the Leven, and all around beneath the rocks; after the drum had beaten tattoo, and the lights of the last ocean-bound steamers had faded out beyond the point of Ardmore.

Then he would skilfully torment himself by recalling all that Mrs. Garth, with the best intentions in the world, had said concerning what Sir Piers would be certain to insist upon and carry out—the union of Mary Montgomerie, the heiress, with his own heir of entail; and well Falconer knew how Sir Piers would view his own slender means and want of family rank. And though he hoped much, he could not know how, in the secrecy of her own room, and in the long hours of 'the stilly night,' Mary treasured the memory of the few precious moments spent in the grotto, and

thought of him and him only—of the influence he had exerted over her when
present, and the memory he had left of
himself when gone.

At times there was in his manner a
passionate dejection, which quite bewildered and provoked the more matter-
of-fact Leslie Fotheringhame.

' 'Pon my soul, old fellow, you're in a
bad way,' the latter sometimes said ; ' you
can't live on this Mary Montgomerie, and
nothing but Mary Montgomerie ! You
must get up a relish for something else
when the drum beats for mess, or we shall
soon have you on the doctor's list.'

So the days and weeks went by till the
middle of March came. Six weeks had
elapsed since he left Eaglescraig—six centuries, apparently, as lovers count their time !

The few words so hastily spoken in the
grotto were deeply graven in his memory,
and graven, too, was the kiss—the unpre-
meditated kiss—pressed so passionately on
her unresisting lips. It seemed to haunt
him with joy, for ever and aye.

'If she loves me, as I know she does,' he often thought, 'I am a fool not to carry her off in defiance of her guardian and all the world. Heaven knows, it is not her fortune I value, but of course that charitable world would think otherwise, though it is entirely in the hands of Sir Piers.'

After the impression made upon him at his departure from Eaglescraig, he felt that he could go back there on no pretence whatever, as no welcome, save from one, would await him, and another invitation would never be accorded. He knew that too well.

Times there were when he threw open his desk, and thought he would write to the general on the subject nearest his heart, at all hazards, and cast himself upon his generosity; and then hope died, and his courage failed, as he remembered his own slender exchequer, his humble rank, apart from his commission, and the general's inordinate pride of birth and value of long descent.

So he dared not write to Eaglescraig,

and from thence came no word, no news,
or sign.

He remembered how Mary had, with
much agitation, interrupted his suggestion
that he should tell Sir Piers of his love for
her. What did she mean, then, unless it
were her dread of the latter's power and
influence over her, and his future plans
with reference to Hew ?

But what would he have thought, what
would his emotions have been, and how
great his indignation, had he known how,
thanks to the malignity and perfidy of
that personage, the good old general, a
mirror of honour himself, viewed him as a
trickster at cards, and a scandal to the
uniform he wore ! Had Falconer been
aware of this circumstance, it would simply
have maddened him; but fortunately for
himself, and the bones of Mr. Hew Caddish
Montgomerie, he knew nothing of it.

He was roused from cogitations such as
these by an order which recalled the detachment to headquarters.

'We start for Edinburgh to-morrow,

Fotheringhame,' he cried, hurrying into his friend's room.

'Hurrah!' responded the latter, springing up; 'thank heaven we are to quit this dull hole! The scenery, of course, is picturesque, and all that sort of thing, but the picturesque is not in my line. The weekly assemblies and all the gaieties are on just now in 'Scotia's darling seat,' and the regimental ball will soon be coming off, so, with genuine satisfaction, I hail the order to rejoin at last. Well, it is a jolly change, anyway.'

And as such, Cecil welcomed it too, though it increased the distance between himself and Eaglescraig, and he could little foresee the calamities that awaited him in Edinburgh, and the crisis that would come in his affairs.

The departure of the detachment was not so duly chronicled in the local prints as its arrival had been; thus Mary knew nothing of Falconer's movements.

In her own heart she fully conceived herself to be engaged—tacitly engaged—to him, and loved to think she was so. Long engagements **are** perilous things, even when the pair **can** see each other at will, or freely correspond, daily or even weekly; tiffs and petty quarrels, **even** little bitternesses, may come to pass that weaken re-gard, unless they be like 'lovers' quarrels, love renewed:' but such a **tie** as that which existed between Falconer and Mary Montgomerie—never hearing of each other, and debarred all correspondence, having only hope for an anchor, was altogether peculiar in its features.

'She is always sad and weary now, Sir Piers,' said Mrs. Garth one day; 'weary at night, and weary at morning, though she tries to conceal it, or deceive us, by occasional bursts of gaiety.'

'Poor little fool! Her mind is still running on that fellow whom I should never have brought to Eaglescraig. But, with all Hew's faults of temper and so forth, she had better think of him and my wishes, Mrs. Garth; so lead her up to it, for that is our *point d'appui,*' replied the general.

'By Jove!' said the amiable Hew, with one of his ugly grimaces, ' she has no more brains than a hen pheasant, I think, to sit as she does all day long looking like a sick monkey.'

Meanwhile Hew was having no better success with his wooing, a fact which was the more perplexing and even harassing now, as he had resigned his Indian Civil Service appointment, and had no dependence, save upon the purse of Sir Piers, who, as the former grudgingly thought, seemed likely to live for ever; and who hoped, and indeed never doubted, that when Mary got over her girlish fancy for Cecil Falconer all things would come right in the end; and to change the scene, as the Edinburgh season was then in its flush, Sir Piers removed his entire household from Eaglescraig to his town residence at the west end of the grey metropolis of the north, a few days after Falconer's detachment had quitted the castle of Dumbarton.

CHAPTER XVIII.

THE CAMERONIANS.

IT was the morning after Cecil Falconer's detachment had come in to headquarters over-night.

In the mess-room about a dozen officers in their blue patrol jackets, all more or less good-looking, even handsome young fellows, each and all having a certain joyous and straightforwardness of manner, were at breakfast, singly or in groups, and all greeted Falconer and Fotheringhame warmly, for both were prime favourites with the corps, and there was much shaking of hands and slapping on the back, with

'Welcome, old fellow!' 'How goes it?' and so forth, while an aroma of coffee and devilled bones pervaded the long room which had windows at each end, and where each officer seemed to be economising time, by reading during the meal, with a daily paper or comic serial—*Punch*, of course—propped against his coffee-pot or sugar-basin. All were discussing the repast in haste, as the hour of morning parade was close at hand.

'Here you are again, Falconer and Fotheringhame!' cried one; 'the Damon and Pythias—the David and Jonathan of the Cameronians! The very men we wanted; you have just come in time for the ball committee!'

'Heard the good news, Falconer, old fellow?' asked Dick Freeport.

'No—what is it? One of the three girls you proposed to accepted you?' said Falconer, leisurely tapping an egg.

'Ah, you've heard that story; nothing so stupid. But is it possible you don't know?'

'What?'

'That your name is in the *Gazette*; but here you are, as large as life,' added Freeport, reading aloud: ' " Lieutenant Cecil Falconer to be Captain, *vice* Brevet Major Balerno seconded for service on the Staff." I congratulate you.'

'And so do we all!' cried Acharn, a frank, jolly captain, though not yet eight-and-twenty.

'Thanks; I knew not that Balerno was leaving us so soon,' said Falconer, whose first thoughts were of Mary Montgomerie.

'This will rouse your spirits,' resumed Freeport.

'Do they want rousing?'

'Well, you looked rather glum last night. Been spoony on some girl in the West, I suppose?'

'Perhaps I was,' replied Cecil, laughing, with a chivalrous idea that to deny his secret love might prove that he was not worthy of it; 'you know that I varied the tedium of country quarters by a visit to the general—old Sir Piers Montgomerie.

But I wish you would fall in love, in downright earnest, yourself, Freeport.'

'What harm have I done you that you should wish me this, Falconer?' asked Dick, drily.

'Any fine girls there—at the general's, I mean?' asked a cheeky young sub, of Falconer, who coloured with annoyance, though the boy—a man in his own estimation and that of fast chums, touting tradesmen and money-lenders—was but a boy after all. 'I have heard that his niece, or grand-niece rather, is a stunner. By Jove, he grows absolutely red! Were you writing verses to her eyebrows, and sighing like a furnace, Falconer?'

'You would have sighed like two or three had ' *you* tried the process,' said Falconer, turning away.

'I do wish you joy, Falconer,' said his friend Fotheringhame, in a low voice; 'and your promotion puts me one step nearer the rank I held when I first knew Annabelle Erroll, and—and—well, played the fool, or worse!'

Cecil thought, would Mary see the *Gazette?* The general, he knew, was certain to do so; and Mrs. Garth too, who read it as regularly as an old Chelsea pensioner; but neither might speak of the event, or deem it wise to revive his name at Eaglescraig.

Falconer was somewhat of a pet among the Cameronians. Excellence in all manly sports ever makes a British officer a favourite with his men; thus, as Falconer could keep a wicket well, was also a prime bowler, a good horseman (though he generally owed his mounts to a friend), and could pull a good oar; moreover, as he joined his men in many a match at tennis, football and shinty, he was popular with them, and the eyes of his company seemed to brighten that morning when he came upon parade, and discipline alone repressed the inclination to give him something like a hearty cheer, and for nearly each and all he had some kind word or inquiry—for the officers and men of a regiment should ever feel as one large family. 'Their hopes and fears are similar,' says a writer; 'their turns of exile will come at the same time. Their good and bad quarters will be enjoyed and endured together, and each one shares, in common with the rest, the proud privilege of perchance some day furnishing in his own person that billet to which, the proverb tell us, every bullet is entitled, or of being "wiped out" by sickness in some pestilential clime, or of going down to the bottom of the sea in some rotten old transport. There is something in their order—a distinctiveness, a speciality about it—which makes them cling together, and stand by one another all the faster; for, although mixing freely with the outer world, there is yet an inner one that is entirely their own.'

All troops like Edinburgh, and the national regiments, from their popularity, more than all. The regimental ball was on the tapis when Falconer and his friend rejoined, and nothing else was spoken of in the fortress, or the gay circle outside it; for the corps, as a national and ancient

one, was deservedly popular in the Scottish
metropolis, the gay season of which is
during the winter, and ends with the
opening of summer—a metropolis where
the people are all devoted to music and
song, and where dancing is a passion with
all classes and ages, so that even a baby
has been taken from its cradle, that the
boast might be fulfilled of *four* generations
being on the floor at once.

'Our regimental hop will be *the* ball of
the season,' said Freeport; 'so I am glad
you have come back, Falconer: the committee could never have done without you.
But once it is over, I fear there will be a
general flight from town, and we shall be
reduced to the melancholy promenade of
the Scottish Academy.'

'Is it open?'

'Yes, with the usual kit-kats of local
nonentities, and the invariable yearly
amount of Bass Rock, Ben Lomond, and
the Water of Leith, without which no
exhibition of pictures here would be complete.'

So Falconer and Fotheringhame were put on the ball committee, and became forthwith immersed in programmes, invitation lists, and interviews with Herr Von Humstrumm, the German bandmaster, the quarter-master and messman.

The castle of Edinburgh may well be deemed the cradle of the Cameronian Regiment, which received its first 'baptism of fire' amid the fierce and protracted siege endured there by the loyal and gallant Duke of Gordon in 1689. The corps, though now Cameronians but in name, have in that title a glorious inheritance of Scottish and military history, that springs from Richard Cameron's bloody grave in lone and wild Airs Moss, where he fell with Bible and sword in hand, in defence of an 'oppressed Kirk and broken Covenant,' and fell bravely, with his face to the enemy, in July, 1680. As a ballad says :

'Oh, weary, weary was the lot of Scotland's true ones
　　then,
　A famine-stricken remnant with scarce the guise of
　　men ;

They burrowed, few and lonely, in the chill, **dark**
    mountain caves,
For those who once had sheltered them were in their
    martyr-graves !'

When the landing of William of Orange
became known in the West of Scotland, a
great body of Cameronians assembled on a
holm near the village of Douglas, in
Lanarkshire, and, to the number of some
thousands, joined the revolted troops who
besieged King James's garrison in Edinburgh Castle during the winter of 1688.
Out of these, two regiments, now re-
spectively the 25th, and 26th or Cameronians, were constituted in the March and
April of the following year. The latter
stipulated that their officers should be
exclusively men 'such as, in conscience,'
they could submit to, as staunch Presby-
terians, and great care was taken in the
selection of them, while an 'elder' was
appointed to every company, so that the
whole battalion should be precisely under
the moral discipline of a parish, and a
Bible formed a part of the necessaries in
every private's knapsack. 'It is impos-

sible,' says the Domestic Annalist of Scotland, 'to read the accounts that are given of this Cameronian Regiment without sympathising with the earnestness of purpose, the conscientious scruples and heroic feeling of self-devotion under which it was established, and seeing in them demonstrations of what is highest and best in the Scottish character.'

Their first colonel was James, Earl of Angus, heir of the lordly line of Douglas, who fell at their head in his twenty-second year, at Steinkirk, but a mullet, or five pointed star, in memory of him, is still one of the badges of the regiment. Their first lieutenant-colonel, Clelland, an accomplished soldier and poet, who had fought under the banner of the Covenant at Drumclog and Bothwell, fell at their head, defending Dunkeld; and their first chaplain was Alexander Shiells, a well-known Scottish divine.

They were clad in red, faced with yellow, the royal colours of Scotland; they wore yellow petticoat-breeches tied below the knee, with monstrous periwigs, and hats of the Monmouth cock, and small Geneva bands at the neck. The captains wore gold-coloured breastplates; those of the lieutenants were of white, and the ensigns of black steel. A proportion of pikemen and halberdiers were in every company, and the bayonets were still cross-hilted daggers, till the socket-bayonet, first adopted by the 25th, or Edinburgh Regiment, was introduced by its colonel, Maxwell, in Flanders.

The Cameronians fought with valour and distinction in the wars of William and Anne; James, Earl of Stair, commanded them in the year of the union, and 1720 saw them at Minorca, under Philip Anstruther of that Ilk, three of whose family have been at their head. Under Preston of Valleyfield they fought valiantly in the American War, and how their major, the unfortunate André, perished is well-known to the historical reader. John Lord Elphinstone led them on the plains of Egypt, and Colonel William Maxwell amid the horrors of the retreat to Corunna. In China, under Colonel Mountain, than whom no better or braver officer ever wore scarlet, they won the dragon which adorns their colours, and the scene of their last active service was amid the arid mountains of Abyssinia. And now, as the Cameronians were originally mustered on the holm of Douglas, they are, at this day, linked in brigade with the Lanarkshire Militia.

Though changed in character and impulse, the regiment is 'the Cameronians' still; but its ranks are no longer manned by the sturdy Covenanters—'men who prayed bare-headed as the troopers of Claverhouse aimed at their hearts—prayed a prayer begun on earth and ended in heaven!'

Local and national regard for the corps caused, we have said, a deep interest to be taken in the forthcoming regimental ball; but, while working on the committee therefor, Cecil Falconer could little foresee the effect that festive occasion was to have on his future career.

He felt his hand actually tremble as he

addressed the invitation cards, handsomely
embossed with the crested sphinx of the
regiment, to Eaglescraig, for the general
and his family. He knew that the former
would be certain to appear, but felt doubts
if Mary Montgomerie would be permitted
to accept for herself; and great was his
surprise and joy when, next day, accept-
ances came promptly from Sir Piers for
Mary, Miss Erroll, and Hew Montgomerie,
dated, not from Eaglescraig, but from the
general's town residence at the west-end of
the city.

She was to be in Edinburgh for the remainder of the season; balls, assemblies,
drums, and parties at which they would be
sure to meet, were before her and Falconer,
and he contemplated the coming weeks as
being pregnant with every enjoyment, with
many a charm and source of pleasure.

And greater would his present joy have
been had he known how Mary treasured
the invitation his hand had addressed, with
a wistful yearning for his presence, for the
pressure of his hands, and the sound of his

love-words over again. For since his
advent at Eaglescraig, Mary had begun a
new existence—a new life of self-devotion
and romance.

CHAPTER XIX.

THE PROGRESS OF EVENTS.

'A COMPANY—I am a captain now!' thought Cecil, as he sat alone in his quarters one evening. Promotion brought him, he hoped, a little nearer *her;* but she was far off from him still, by her surroundings and the influences that were brought to bear upon her.

He recalled the words of a writer who says: 'When a young man wants to marry a girl, he has already made up his mind that she is worthy of him, otherwise he would not wish to marry her. The next thing to do is to make a rigid cross-examination of himself, and see whether *he* is worthy of her.' Falconer did so, and, of course, deemed himself immeasurably the inferior of Mary, but more than all in worldly prospects and even social position, albeit that he was now a captain of the Cameronians; and yet only that evening, in the mess-room, he had heard rattling Dick Freeport say, that it was 'the duty of every man wearing a red coat to hook an heiress, if he wanted one.'

He looked around the room in which he sat, his 'quarters,' and smiled, in spite of himself, as he mentally contrasted its appurtenances—its 'fixings,' as the Americans say—with such as were deemed absolutely necessary to the existence of one so refined as Mary Montgomerie, and he began to surmise whether or not his love was a selfish one.

The bare floor, scrubbed, however, as clean as his servant, Tommy Atkins, could make it; the walls white-washed, and liable to impart their tint to everything that came in contact with them; a couple

of Windsor chairs ; a table liable to unpleasant collapses, especially if sat upon, as
it often was ; an iron camp-bed, wherein to
dream of Mary and glory, with a strip of
carpet, as a luxury, by its side ; a wash-
stand that took the form of a square box
when the route came ; a tin tub, tilted up
on end in a corner ; an iron coal-box, or
scuttle, royally marked with ‘V.R.’ and an
imperial crown ; a fire-grate full of torn
billets and cigar-ends ; a rack containing
sticks, whips, a couple of swords ; a little
narrow mantelpiece, littered with pipes,
cigars, and havanna boxes ; but no flowers,
and not a single pretty knickknack suggestive of female influences were there. Destitute of all ornament, it was essentially a
man's apartment—a very barrack-room.

Yet some feminine memorials of ‘auld
lang syne’ were not wanting ; for in Cecil's
most secret repositories were the treasured
letters of his mother, her photos, a lock
of her dark hair, thickly silvered with
white, and a bunch of withered daisies that
he had gathered on her grave, which she

had found in a distant land—mementoes
treasured all the more that the story of her
life had been a sad one.

If the interior of Cecil's apartment was
plain to excess, the view from its windows
was second to none in the world. On one
side, far down below, spread the Edina of
the Georgian and Victorian ages; on the
other towered up Dunedin, grey and grim,
in all the dead majesty of a grand, historical, and royal past—the Dunedin of
battle and siege, yet instinct with life and
vitality in all its pulses still; and far, far
away, to where the golden sun was setting
at the gates of the west, spread the wondrous landscape, till the green Ochil ranges
and the pale blue cone of Ben Lomond,
sixty miles distant, closed it in.

And anon, when darkness falls, more
wondrous still is the beauty of the scene
when the broken masses and spiky ridges
of the old town sparkle with ten thousand
lights. 'High in air a bridge leaps the
chasm between,' wrote one who knew it
well; 'a few emerald lamps, like glow-

worms, are moving about in the railway station below, while a solitary crimson one is at rest. That ridged bulk of blackness, with splendour bursting out at every pore, is the wonderful Old Town where Scottish history mainly transacted itself, while opposite the modern Princes Street is blazing throughout its length. During the day the castle looks down upon the city, as if out of another world ; stern with all its peacefulness, its garniture of trees, its slopes of grass. The rock is dingy enough in colour, but after a shower its lichens laugh out greenly in the returning sun, while the rainbow is brightening on the lowering sky beyond. How deep the shadow which the castle throws at noon over the gardens at its feet, where the children play ! How grand when giant bulk and towering crown blacken against the sunset !'

Gazing dreamily from his window, Cecil sat lost in thought, with a note in his hand —the acceptance to the ball invitation—a note written, he knew, by the hand of

Mary, and which he had rescued from Dick Freeport, who was sacrilegiously about to tear and toss it into the waste-paper basket; and at the time we may suppose that our lover felt as Sir Robert Cotton did when he rescued the original Magna Charta from the shears of the Cockney tailor, who was about to cut it into yard-measures for doublets and trunk hose.

But Cecil roused himself when the drums beat on the slope below the citadel gate, and donning his mess-dress, he betook him to the dinner-table, where the trophied silver plate added splendour to luxury.

'So, as the general is in town, you'll leave a card, of course, Falconer,' said Fotheringhame, with a peculiar smile, as Cecil took a seat by his side.

'I am in duty bound to do so; though, sooth to say,' added Falconer, for their confidences had become mutual, 'the coldness that accompanied my departure from Eaglescraig gives me unpleasant doubts of my reception; yet leave a card, of course, I must.'

Then he thought of Mary on the morning he came away, and the farewell wave of her handkerchief.

'If I call, Fotheringhame, won't you accompany me?'

'Thanks; no. Old fellow, you forget.'

'What?'

'That Miss Erroll's acceptance for the ball came from the general's house.'

'A pleasant place it will be to visit,' said Dick Freeport, striking into the conversation from the opposite side of the table. 'I have had Falconer's confidential report on the subject; he states that the general's cellar is excellent, the sherry pale and dry, the old port full-bodied, the Chateau Lagrange unequalled, and Moët's Imperial ditto! His cook is a regular French *chef*, with a salary that exceeds the pay of Sir Piers himself, no doubt; and then there is his ward——'

'Halt, Dick! how your tongue runs on!' said Cecil, with some annoyance. 'His ward is not to be lightly spoken of at any mess-table—ours especially.'

'I saw the general's carriage to-day in George Street,' cried a cheeky sub-lieutenant from the lower end of the table. 'I knew it by the coat-of-arms; and, by Jove, there were two stunning girls in it!'

'Miss Montgomerie and her friend Miss Erroll, no doubt,' said Fotheringhame. 'One dark—a brunette, and the other brilliantly fair?'

'Exactly; I took stock of them both. Dick will be bringing his engagement-ring with the blue stone into action now.'

As this was a regimental joke it caused a little laugh, amid which Acharn, the sporting man of the corps, came in hastily in his mess-jacket and vest, looking rather grim and cross.

'Late for mess, old man,' said Fotheringhame. 'What is up, eh?'

'Wine!' said Acharn sharply, to a waiter, and then replied: 'Only that I am rather up a tree just now.'

'You are rather fond of climbing,' said Fotheringhame. 'Is it lofty?'

'Lofty as a Himalayan pine, by Jove!

I say, Falconer, you were at the general's place, Eaglescraig—or what's its name ?'

' Yes.'

' Was there a fellow named Hew Montgomerie there ?'

' Yes.'

' Hew Caddish Montgomerie, as his pasteboard has it—he is well named ! and from whom you won at cards ?'

' No ; but who utterly rooked *me* at cards !' said Falconer angrily, while he and Fotheringhame exchanged glances.

' Well, I met him at the United Service Club this afternoon, though he is not a member. We somehow got into play, and I have lost enough to make my governor pull a very long face when he comes to hear of it—a cool £500. He is a fellow whose shifty eyes and thin lips often smile, but never in unison ?'

' I know that his face never wears an expression of manly truth—for truth isn't in him !' said Falconer.

' The fellow is a downright cad, I understand,' said Fotheringhame ; ' he will go to

the devil with the down-train, and never
know how to put on the breaks. Why
were you fool enough to play with a
stranger?'

'And lose?' said Acharn, twisting his
thick black moustache.

'By all accounts it would be a miracle if
you *won.*'

'He has promised me my revenge to-
morrow.'

'At what game was it you lost £500?'
asked Fotheringhame.

'At roulette, piquet, and écarté; but
most at écarté.'

'By Jove! I should think so,' said Falconer, remembering Hew's 'mild play.'
'Why didn't you look under the table?' he
asked in a low voice.

'For what?' exclaimed Acharn, with
surprise.

'The cards he was dropping unknown to
you.'

'Good heavens, do you say so!'

'Why, the fellow's a regular leg!' said

Fotheringhame; but Falconer contented himself by saying:

'Your promised revenge will never come. Next time he asks you to play, decline, and say you do so by my advice—*mine*—don't forget.'

Acharn did so, and the fact did not increase Master Hew's goodwill to Falconer; but little indeed could the latter guess how the good old general had been led to view *him*.

A favourite with the entire regiment he was known to be, even to the very school-children; thus it was with some surprise the commanding-officer, some days after, heard the remarks of the general at the club, made privately to himself, however.

'I have to thank you, Sir Piers,' said the lieutenant-colonel, 'for extending the hospitality of your house to one of the best of my officers.'

'Best—the smartest, perhaps you mean?' said Sir Piers, coldly.

'Smartest and best!' replied the lieutenant-colonel, emphatically.

'Sorry to hear it, sir ; sorry to hear it. When we were cantonned at Jodpore——'

'Excuse me, Sir Piers; but I do not understand.'

'He is too fond of cards, sir—too fond of cards for my taste, sir.'

'I never saw a card in his hand!' persisted the other.

'Strange!'

The lieutenant-colonel thought these remarks more than strange, too; but Sir Piers did not choose to inform him of Hew's malevolent reports, and plunged at once into sundry reminiscences of Jodpore and its Rajpoots.

Mary would certainly be the queen of the forthcoming regimental ball, and Falconer was full of the most delightful anticipations concerning it.

'Leslie Fotheringhame will be there!' was the secret thought of Annabelle Erroll; 'how *are* we to meet? As strangers? Would that I had not come to Edinburgh at all—and yet!'

Yet—what? She scarcely knew.

Mary was in full anticipation also of the ball—its joys and its brilliance, and nightly laid her head on the pillow to sleep and dream, if she could, of a region where all was romance, light and splendour, bands of music, festooned banners and brilliant uniforms, with one central figure—Cecil Falconer!

CHAPTER XX.

THE OLD STORY AGAIN.

IT may easily be supposed that Cecil Falconer did not lose much time in paying what was to pass ostensibly as a ceremonious visit to Sir Piers Montgomerie's family. Evening parade was over, when he quitted the fortress in a carefully assorted suit of mufti, and betook him to the northwestern quarter of the New Town, in one of the most fashionable streets of which stood the stately house of the general, in a situation of wonderfully picturesque beauty, overlooking the deep ravine through which the Leith flows under a noble bridge of three arches, each of which is ninety-six feet in span.

On one side stands an ancient tolbooth, with crow-stepped gables; on the other, a steep green bank crowned by a beautiful church and stately crescent. Between these yawns the rocky ravine, wherein lie an old bridge of other days, and a cluster of quaint mills and dwellings, and the river roaring in snow-white foam over a broad and lofty weir; the whole place having in all its features a marvellous resemblance to the Spanish village of Banos in Leon.

And now, when Falconer stood upon the threshold of the mansion, there flashed upon his mind the recollection that on this very day it was that his father and mother had both died—the latter on the anniversary of the former's demise, eighteen years before; thus he doubted whether he had chosen a fortunate time, for it has truly been said, that there are certain moods of the human mind in which we cannot help ascribing 'an ominous importance to any remarkable coincidence wherein things of

moment are concerned;' and he was in this
mood then.

In obedience to the sonorous bell, the
double-door was thrown open, revealing one
of those spacious entrance-halls peculiar to
Scottish houses, with tiger-skins—some of
Sir Piers' Indian spoils—and Persian rugs
covering the length of its tesselated floor,
and marble pedestals with tall Chinese and
Japanese vases standing on either side.

The general had gone to his club, in
Queen Street; Mrs. Garth and Miss Erroll
were out in the carriage, but were expected
back soon; Miss Montgomerie was at
home. So said the valet, who remembered
Falconer, and smiled a welcome to him, but
said nothing of the whereabouts of Hew,
who was a favourite with none.

Mary was then at home, and perhaps
alone, so Cecil's heart beat lightly and
happily as he was ushered into the stately
double drawing-room, which had hangings
of rose-coloured silk laced with white,
and was stately with crystal chandeliers,
venetian mirrors, cabinets of rare china,

statuettes, and gems of art in the way of pictures and jars, amid which the eyes of Falconer saw only Mary Montgomerie—Mary seated near an antique tripod table, whereon was set out the dainty Wedgewood china for five o'clock tea, and varying her time between knitting soft woollen socks for some old cotter of Eaglescraig, and gazing from the window on the buds of spring that were bursting in the warm sunshine, and the sweet flowers that made the parterres gay; but she started from her chair when the servant announced,

'Captain Falconer.'

She repeated the name mechanically, and grew very pale as she presented her hand.

'Do not call me "captain,"' urged Cecil, retaining it, while the thoughts of both went naturally back to their last meeting in the grotto, and the avowal made then; and Mary grew shy in manner, for she had been haunted by a dread lest her wave of the handkerchief to Cecil on his departure from Eaglescraig had been unladylike, though Annabelle assured her that, after all that had passed, any young girl would have done precisely the same.

'But you *are* a captain now,' she said, smiling; 'and I congratulate you upon the circumstance. It has given me real pleasure, you may be well assured.'

'I thank you, from my heart,' replied Cecil, and she withdrew her hand, while he was longing to take up the links of the old story, gathering even courage from the omen that Snarley, in a new blue and silver collar, with his mistress's monogram and a bell, barked, whimpered, and frisked about him with delight.

Snarley had an undoubted propensity for worrying rats in the stable court, under the auspices of Hew Montgomerie and Pate Pastern, the head-groom; also proclivities for the kitchen and low life generally: but here he was in the drawing-room to welcome the visitor.

'You knew I would call?' said Falconer, after a pause.

'I — hoped you would,' said Mary, timidly.

'You did!' he exclaimed in a low voice, as he started to her side. 'Oh, my darling!'

'Yes—of course,' replied Mary faintly, and blushing deeply now, as he took both her hands in his and gazed into her eyes with passionate tenderness; and somehow it came speedily to pass that as they stood so near, they were posed like the Black Brunswicker and his love, or the Huguenot and his guardian angel, in the well-known pictures; but if the pose was delicious, the speeches that accompanied it were a little fatuous and incoherent.

After a time, Falconer, still holding her in his embrace and gazing tenderly into her upturned eyes, made the somewhat prosaic request:

'You will keep some round dances for me at the ball, of course, darling?'

'Gladly would I do so, dearest Cecil— but——'

'But what, Mary love?'

'I am under such supervision—Hew, for instance——'

'It is intolerable!' said Falconer, as a gesture of impatience escaped him. 'To love you, and say that I love you, dearest Mary, means views of marriage, and the hope that you will be mine—mine for ever, sweetest pet,' he continued, with infinite tenderness of tone and manner, taking her little face between his hands, after the mode of the pictured Huguenot; but Mary partially and nervously withdrew from him. 'You are free, Mary, are you not?' he asked, with great and sudden anxiety.

There was no answer, and she seemed intently studying the pattern of the carpet.

'You are not, you cannot be, engaged!' he exclaimed in a low and earnest voice, and dreading some change since they parted.

'No, certainly—not of my own free will,' was her curious reply, while tears trembled on her dark lashes.

'How then?'

'Mrs. Garth told you all, did she not?'

' Do you know your own mind, Mary?'
he asked, taking her caressingly in his
arms.

' Yes,' said she, with a sob in her
throat.

' How is it to be, then?'

There was no answer.

' Mary!'

She could scarcely have made any reply
just then, as Cecil closed her sweet lips
most effectually.

' Hew actually takes his position with
me for granted,' said she, after a little
pause, with her head reclined on Cecil's
shoulder. ' He is absurd, and insolent as
a wooer, yet seems to think there is no
need for exerting himself to win a bride
that is bestowed upon him. He treats me
as if I were his property—a gift from Sir
Piers in fact,' she continued with an angry
little laugh.

' And you, with all your beauty and
wealth too, Mary, are to become the
sacrifice of an old man's ambition to endow
his house, and a young man's avarice! Oh,

my darling, it is monstrous ! and in this age of the world, ridiculous too ! But perhaps the good old general may come round in time, and see the folly of his scheme.'

She shook her head, and said brokenly :

' You speak of wealth—I would I were penniless, for your sake ; it is as a millstone about my neck ; I think papa's will was most iniquitous !'

Until Mary Montgomerie met and knew Cecil Falconer, she had lived like the lady of Shalott, in a world of dreams—a young girl's dreams of a lover ; for even the advent of Hew as an admirer—an intended —had certainly not embodied the idea to her.

She had read in Byron that a woman's love was a woman's whole existence, and such she would have made it now to herself ; and doubtless had Cecil chosen to exert the power he had over her heart, and lured her, as one less scrupulous might have done, into risking the *esclandre,* he would have persuaded her to defy Sir

Piers and fly with him ; but he never for a moment entertained the idea of a measure that would have been such injustice to herself, as it would have involved the loss of her fortune, and perhaps its eventual transference to Hew !

Snarley now suddenly showed his teeth, as if to announce the approach of the latter through the outer drawing-room, where it would almost seem that he had been again an unseen listener, as at Eagles-craig.

' *Petit chien !*' exclaimed Mary, as the Huguenot pose was suddenly relinquished, and she snatched up her dog to kiss it ; ' *petit chien*—dear wee doggie, don't be jealous of—oh, it's *you*, Hew—how tiresome !' she added under her breath, as that personage lounged upon the scene, and drily gave his cold, fishy hand to Falconer.

' Hew again !' thought Mary with a shiver of repugnance ; and again, as in the instance of the grotto, she marvelled, with intense annoyance, how much he had

overseen and overheard, and how long he
had been *en perdue!*

Nearly ignoring the presence of Falconer,
who assumed his hat and gloves, he bowed
coldly and said curtly :

'I am about to have a canter down
Granton way : will you join me, Mary ?'

'I would rather be excused.'

'Why ?'

'It is anything but a pretty road—all
stone walls and no trees.'

Hew scowled. The answer showed
plainly that his company would not com-
pensate for the dulness of the road—'and
before that fellow Falconer, too !'

'Annabelle will go, perhaps.'

'She is out with the old soldier, Mrs.
Garth.'

'Hew !' she exclaimed, while with
curiously-mingled emotions of delight and
annoyance, Falconer, deeming that the
time had come to depart, bowed himself
out as Hew rang the bell.

'Ha !' thought the latter, 'she will not
ride with me, and she has not driven out

with them, so she expected this fellow!
They have some secret understanding unknown to Sir Piers, most certainly. But
they have not yet come to the third volume
of their little romance!'

Mary read his thoughts and suspicions
in his face, and her heart swelled with
anger.

'We must stop this nonsense, Hew—or
you must, I mean,' said she abruptly, and
with flashing eyes.

'Stop it?'

'Yes, as I mean to be the mistress of my
own actions; and the sooner your inter-
ference with me ends, the better for us both.'

'What do you mean?'

'What I say, sir!' replied Mary desperately, and with tears in her eyes as she
swept from the room; for though she de-
ferred to the years and affection of Sir
Piers, she was resolved *now* to have neither
mercy nor toleration for Hew, who eyed
her malevolently as she withdrew.

Sweet indeed had been the love-passage

between these two—Cecil and Mary—
knitting their hearts closer together. Affection had been ensured to the full and
been accepted to the full; but no promise
had been given, and the future was vague
as ever.

Cecil had a species of rival in Hew,
certainly; but one that, strange to say,
provoked no jealousy, anger, or sense of
suspicion, though there were the influence
and authority of Sir Piers to dread, together with what might be their ultimate
result upon the gentle nature of Mary,
who might be bent to accept the fate intended for her, as being but a portion of
the inevitable. Besides, if the regiment
were ordered suddenly abroad, the chances
of their ever meeting again would be faint
and few indeed.

Though Hew, as we have already indicated, had no genuine love for Mary, he
fully appreciated the wonderful beauty of
her person, and endorsed to the full the
general's desire that he should marry her,
and a creditable wife indeed she would be

to the future baronet of Eaglescraig ; thus his piqued self-esteem and his avarice rendered him secretly savage that he made worse than no progress with her in his wooing. He felt as if placed in rather a ridiculous position with his patron ; and thus the whole tide of his venom flowed towards the innocent Falconer, though the appearance of the latter on the scene had not changed in the least degree Mary's views of him—Hew Montgomerie.

There was no open quarrel between the latter and Falconer, but each had a very decided repugnance to the other, and the soldier knew and felt him to be his secret enemy ; and in their chance intercourse in public places and at the U. S. club, whither he came under the general's wing, the **veiled** hatred of Hew grew deeper as he felt **instinctively** that he was every way, in tone, in bearing, **and** in mind, the inferior of Falconer.

He became more **than** usually boorish, for about this time he had **a** curious run of ill-luck in his turf speculations ; ' straight tips ' had turned out the reverse of straight ; ' good things ' on coming events had turned out badly too ; he had been jockied and wanted money sorely, having lost in a few hours all that he had won from Acharn, while the latter, instead of proposing to have his revenge, mentioned incidentally ' his friend Falconer,' and declined all play ; the next time Acharn cut him *dead*, and he began to find all players avoiding him.

Though Mrs. Garth was invaluable as a chaperon, such a guardian is not so necessary in the streets of ' the Queen of the North' as in those of the sister metropolis ; consequently Mary could go abroad alone whenever she chose, while curiously enough she seemed to have lost all taste for the use of the carriage now.

END OF VOL. I.

BILLING AND SONS, PRINTERS AND ELECTROTYPERS, GUILDFORD.

J. W. & Sons.